Fantastical Dragons
COLORING BOOK

Aaron Pocock

Dover Publications
Garden City, New York

This exciting coloring book features thirty-one detailed illustrations of that most legendary of creatures, the dragon. Fantasy lovers will treasure these images of the mighty beasts aloft in the sky, asleep in a forest glade, and protecting beautiful maidens, along with many other dramatic scenes. Intended especially for the advanced colorist, these images will help your imagination soar. In addition, the pages are perforated and are printed on one side only for easy removal and display.

Bibliographical Note

Fantastical Dragons Coloring Book is a new work, first published
by Dover Publications in 2017.

International Standard Book Number

ISBN-13: 978-0-486-81269-4

ISBN-10: 0-486-81269-3

Manufactured in the United States by LSC Communications Book LLC
81269311   2021
www.doverpublications.com

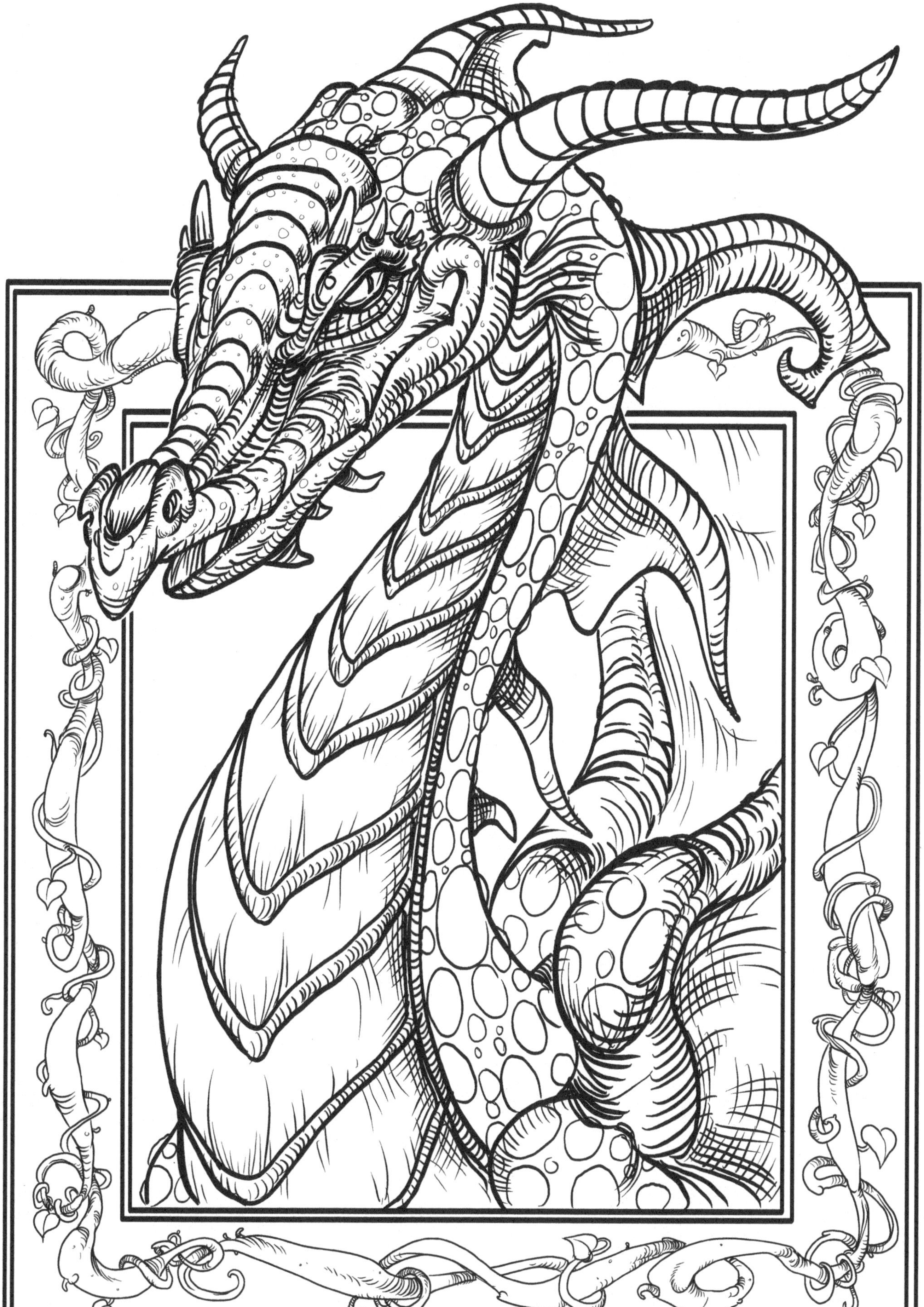

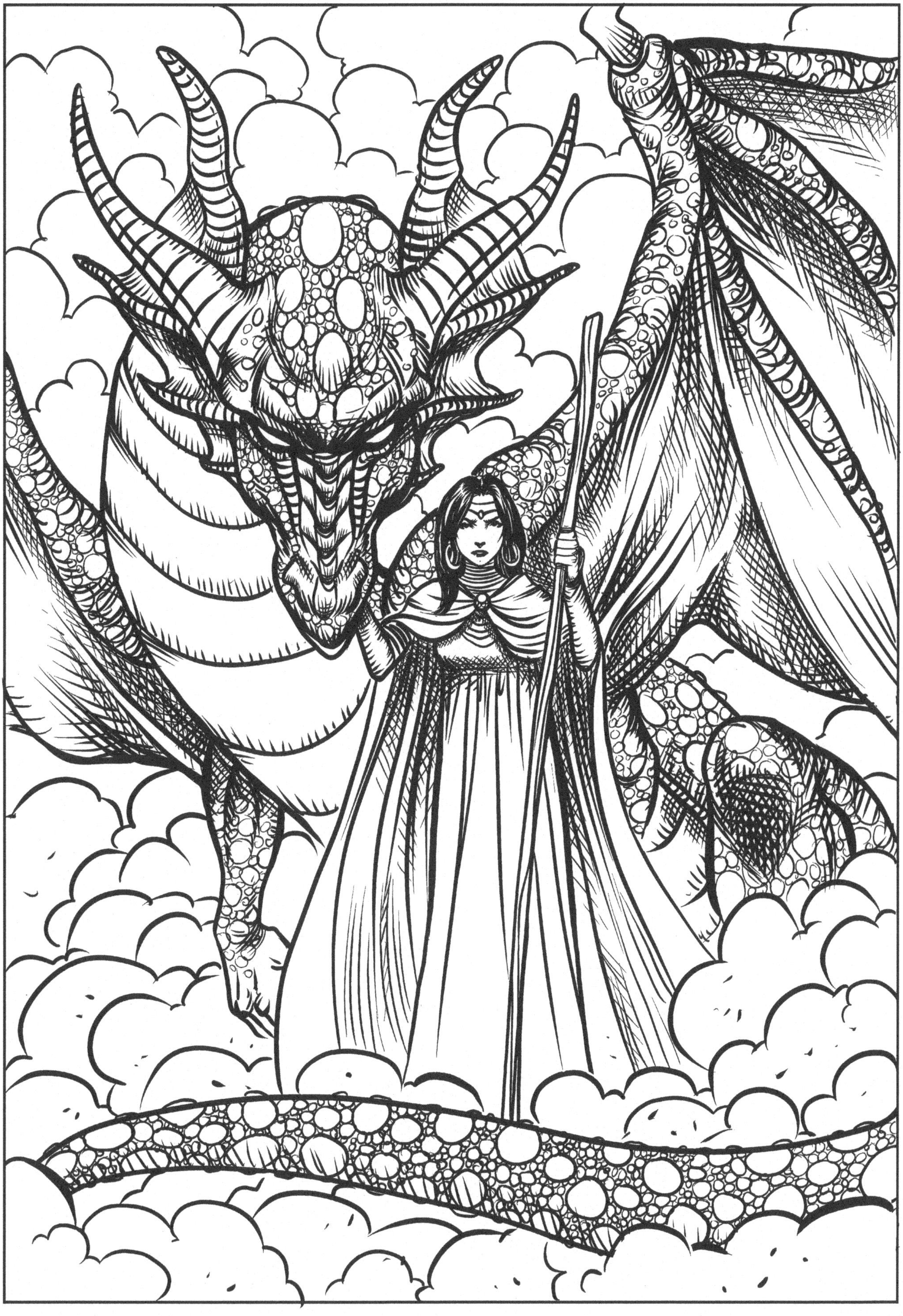

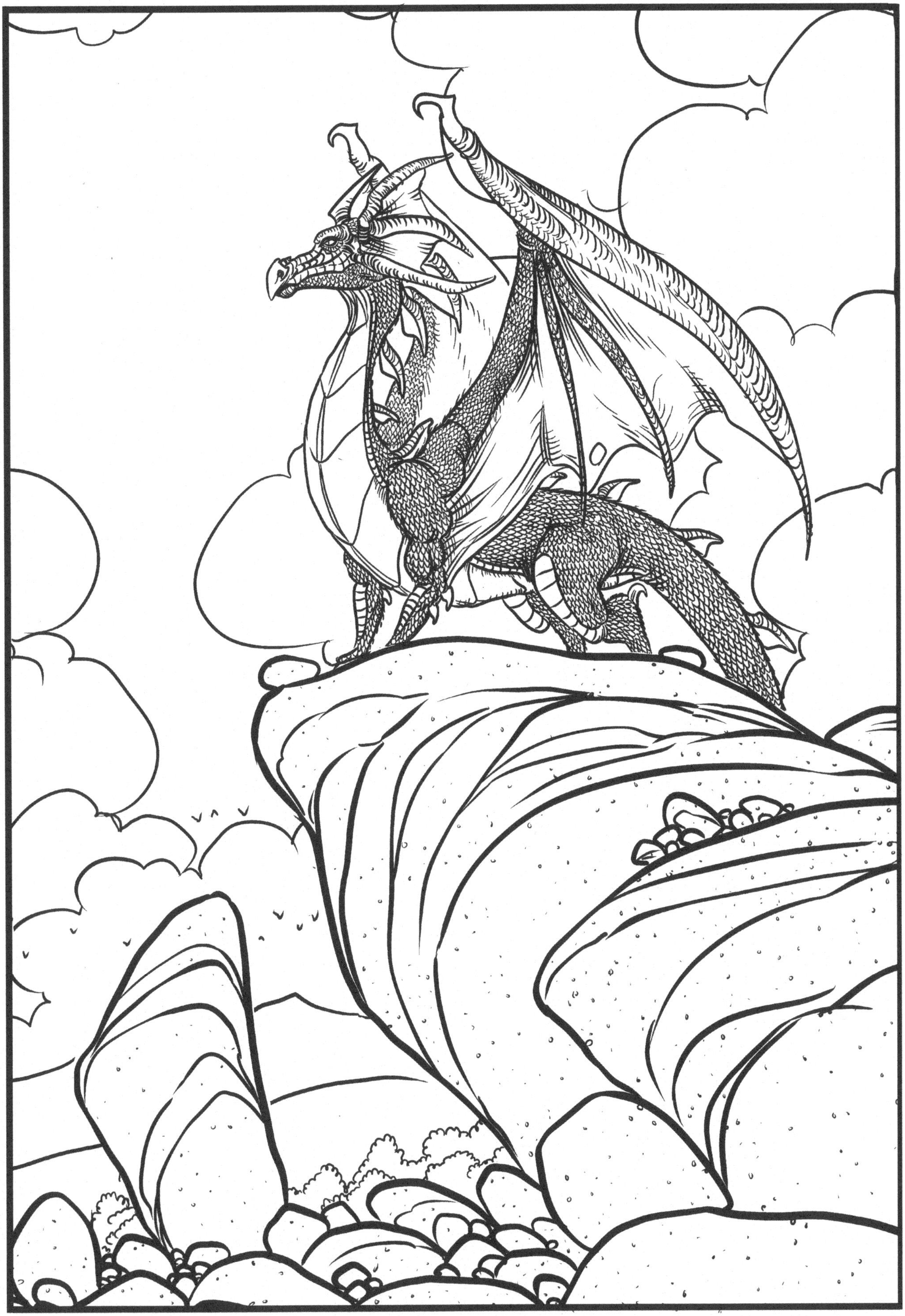

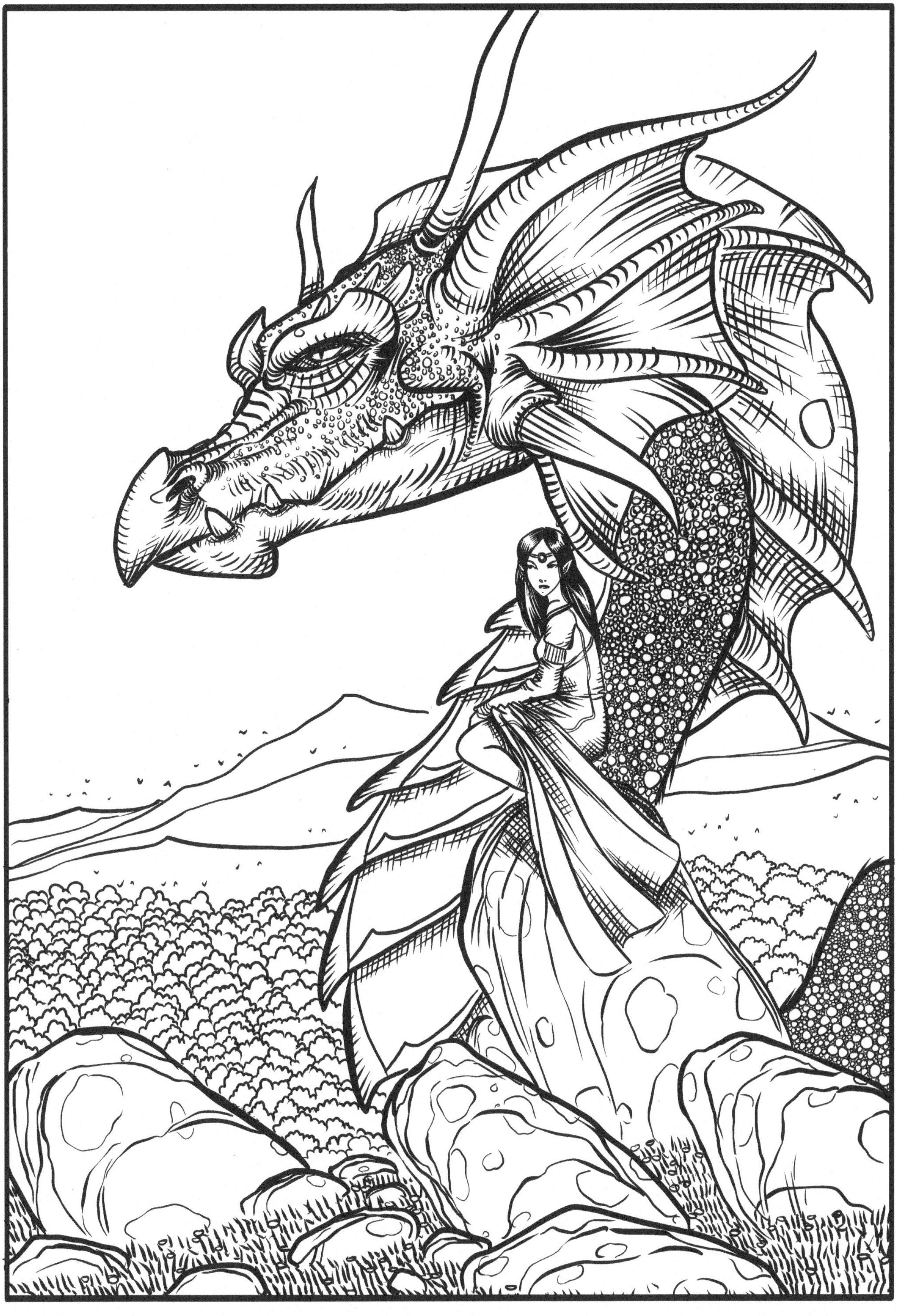

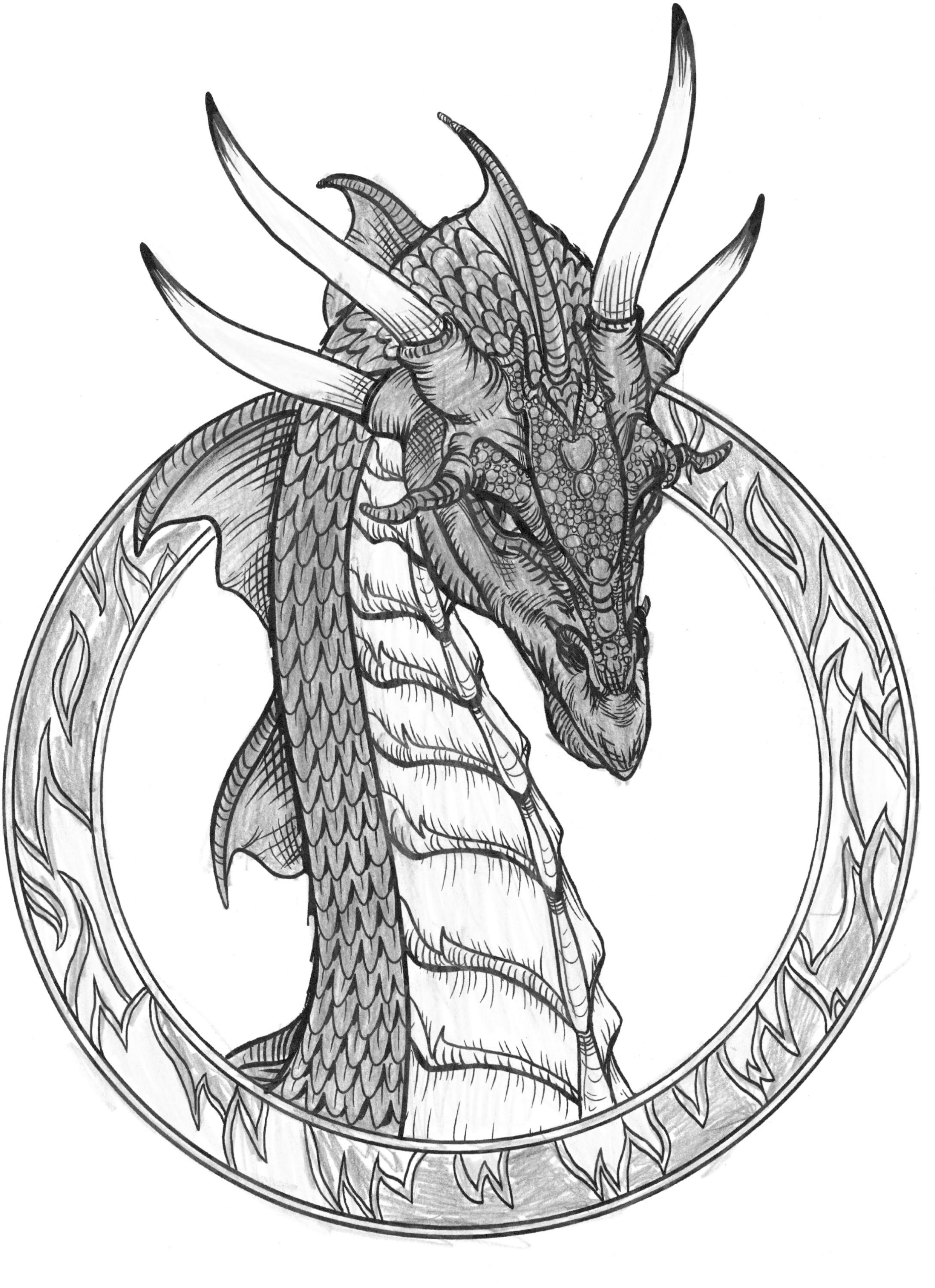

93VSESKQ
z55NYRUC

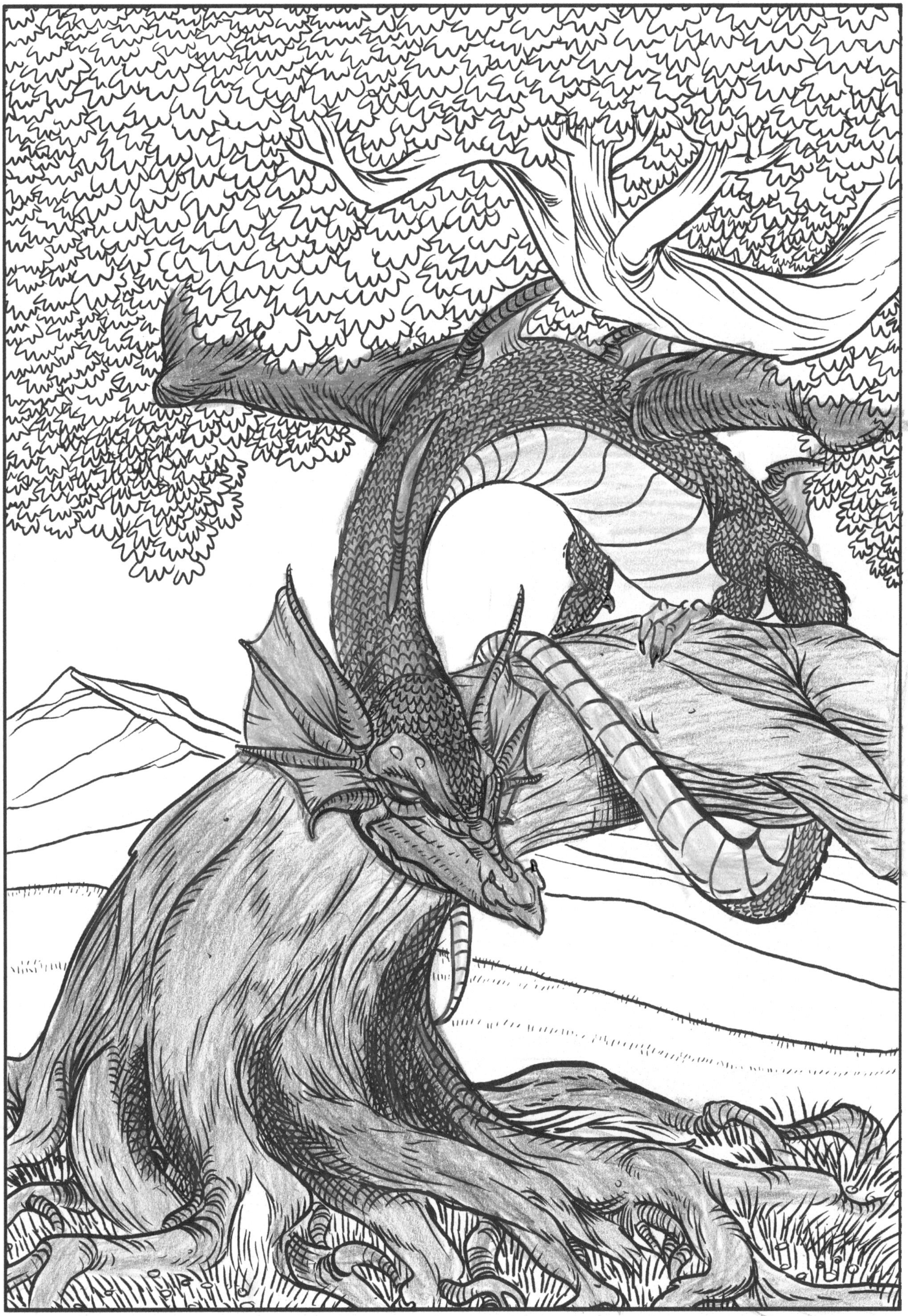

Burnt Sienna

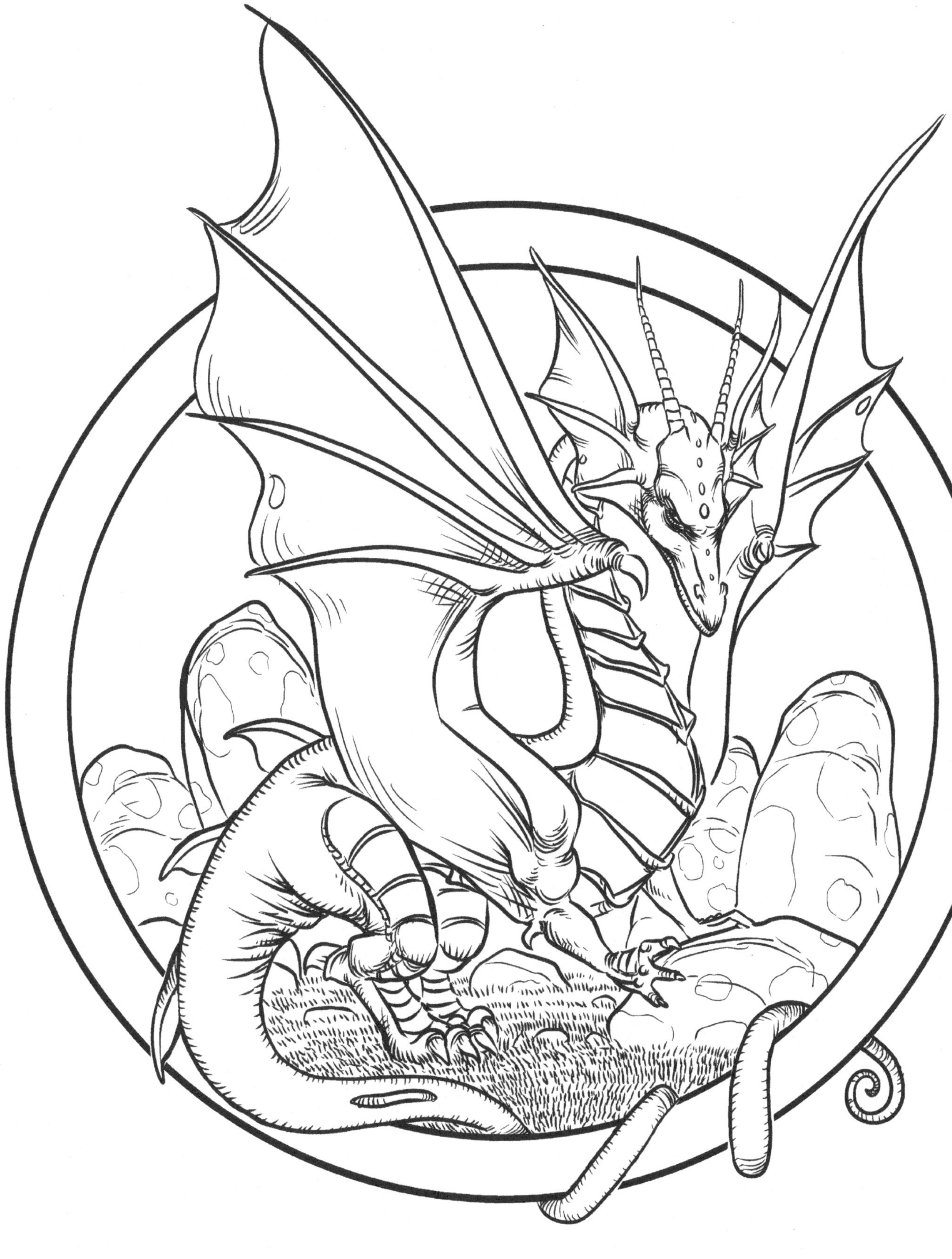

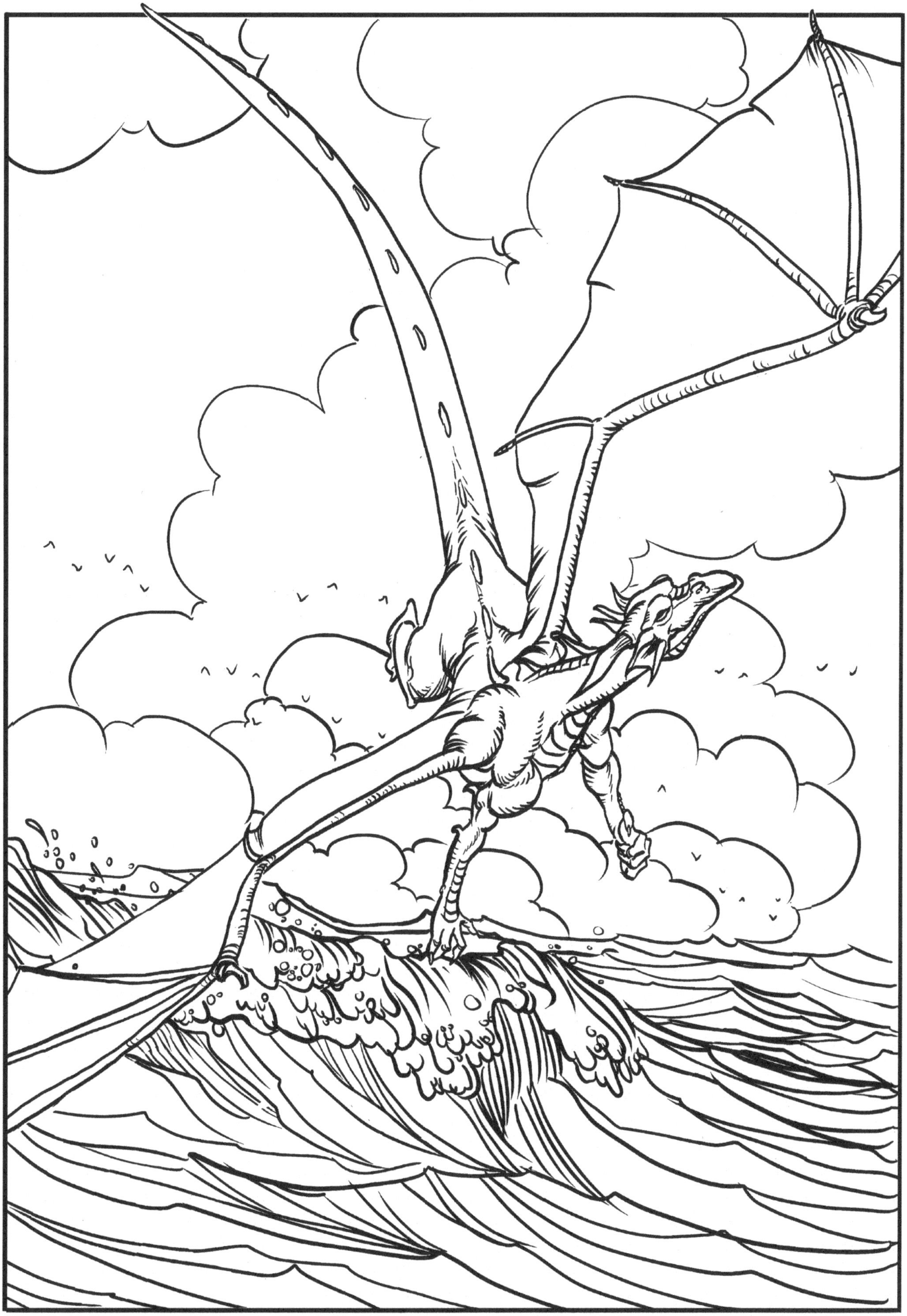

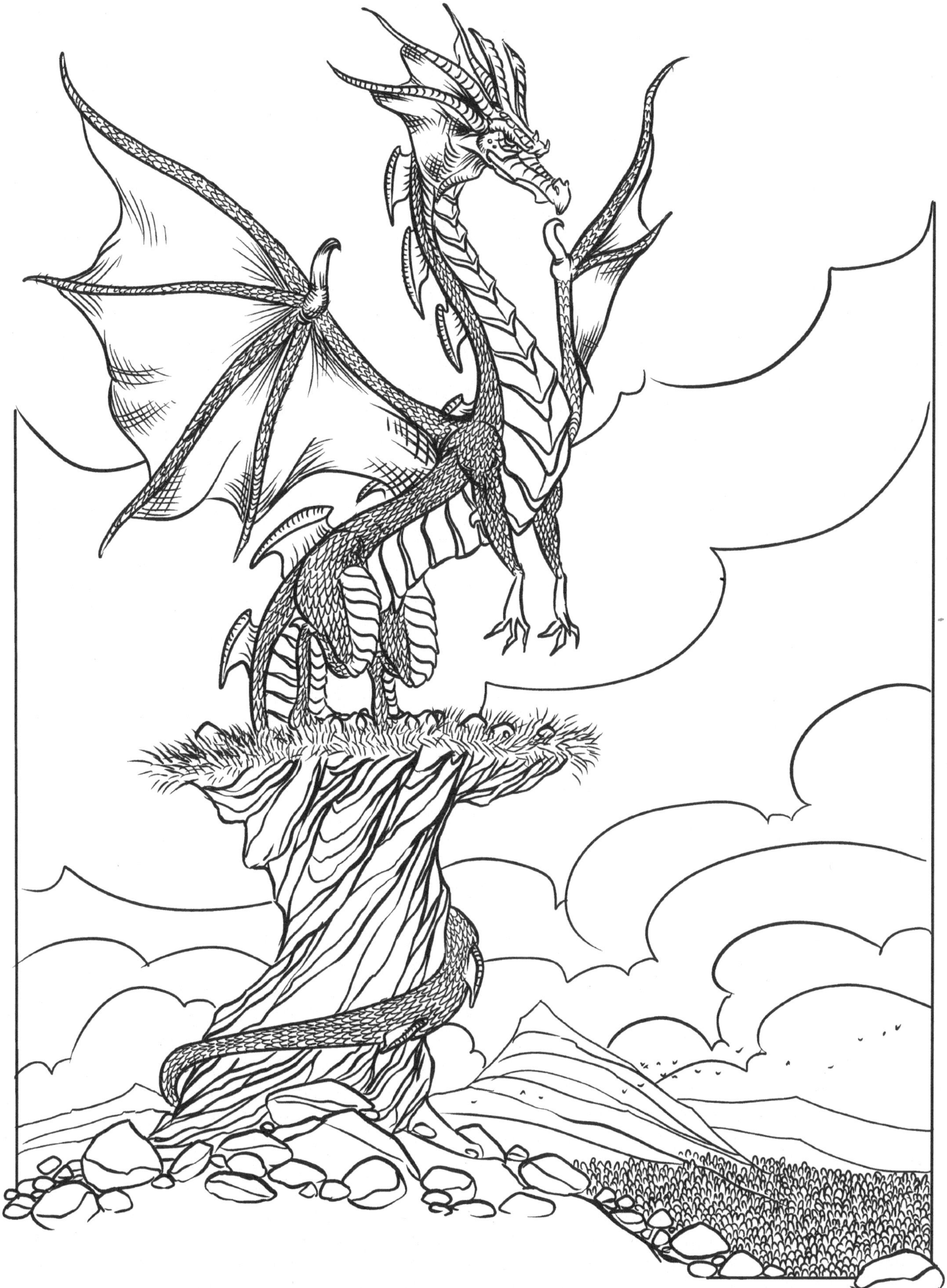

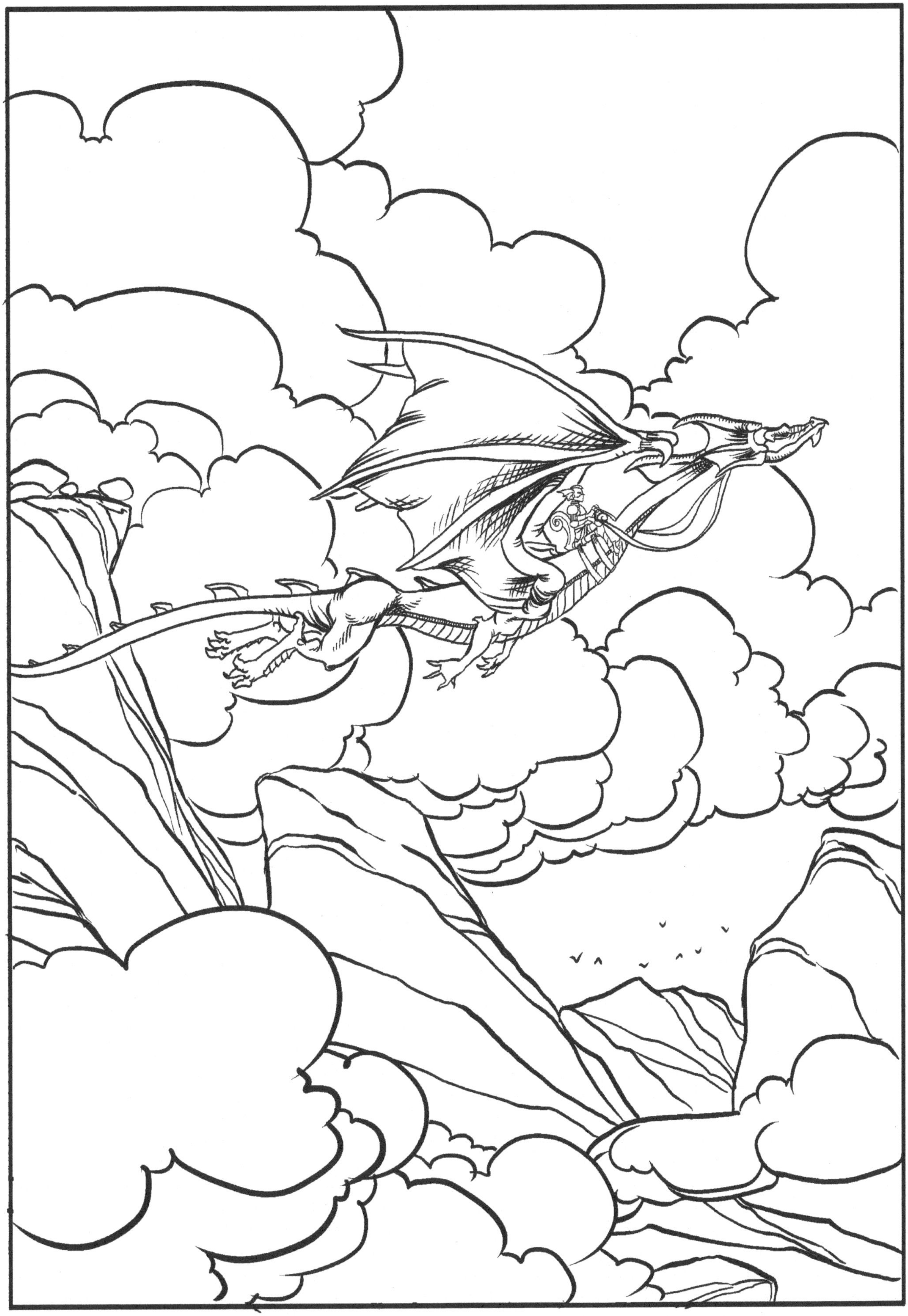

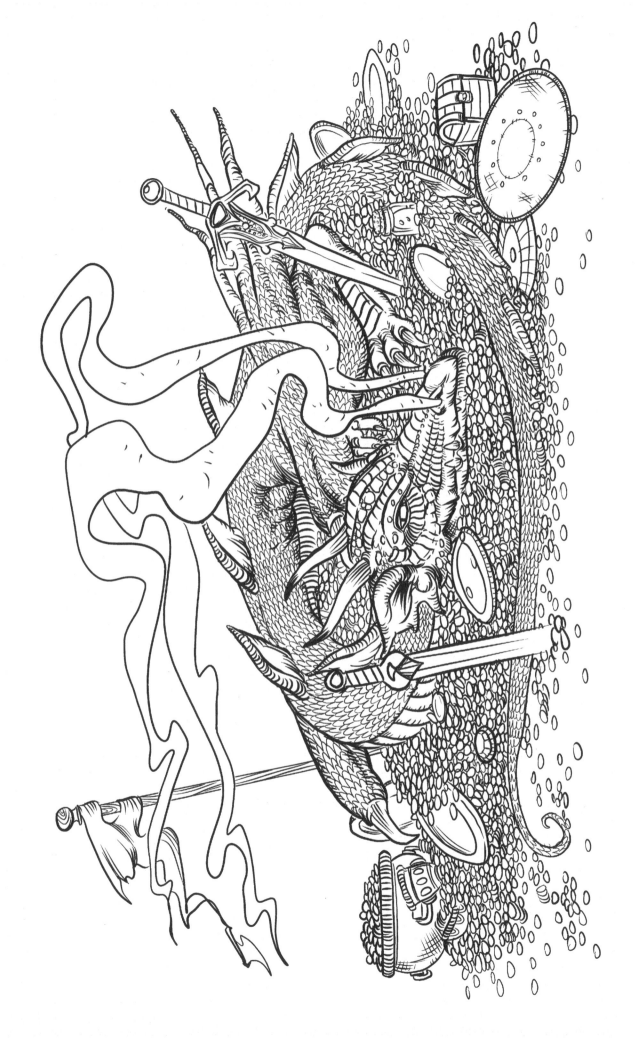

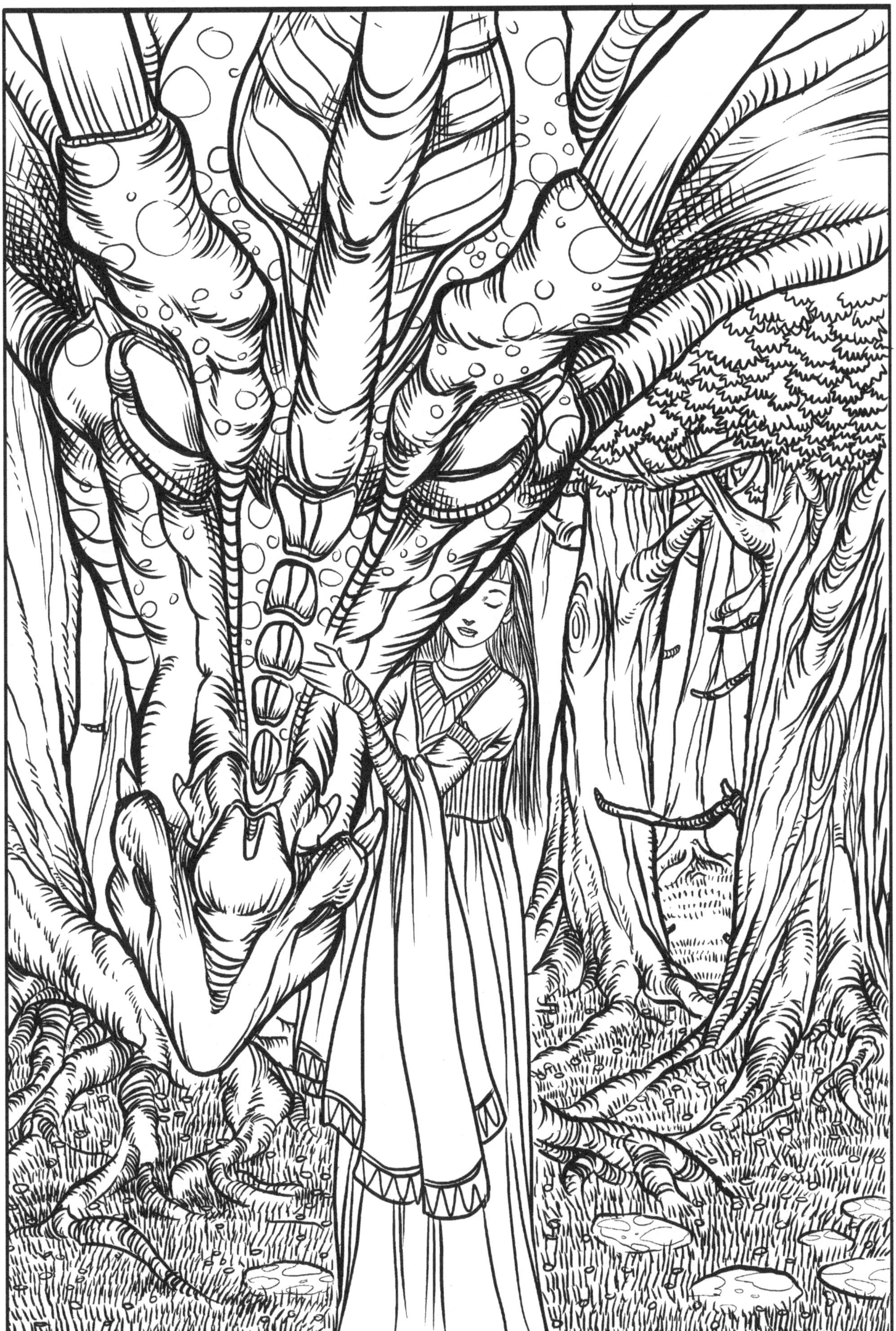

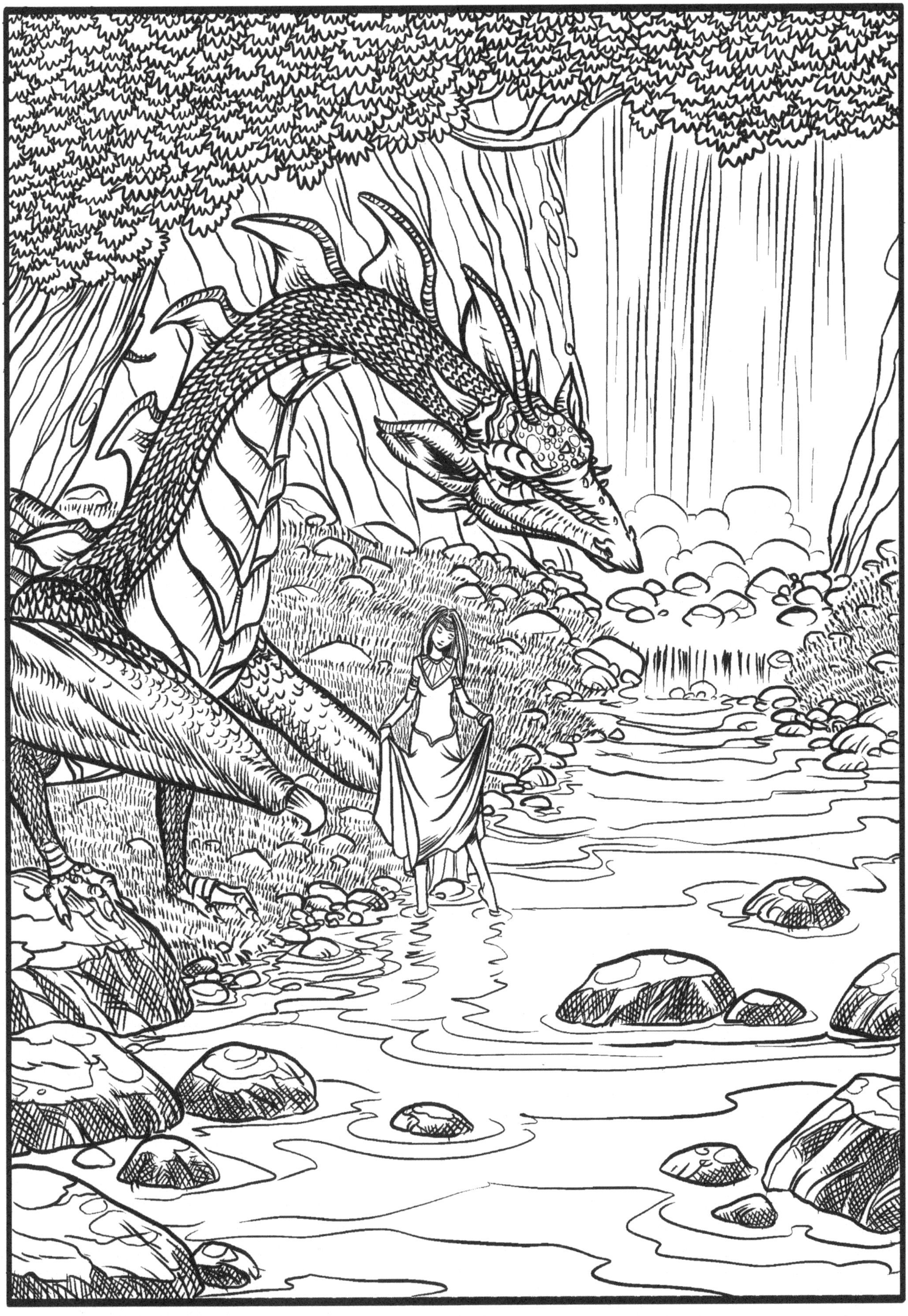

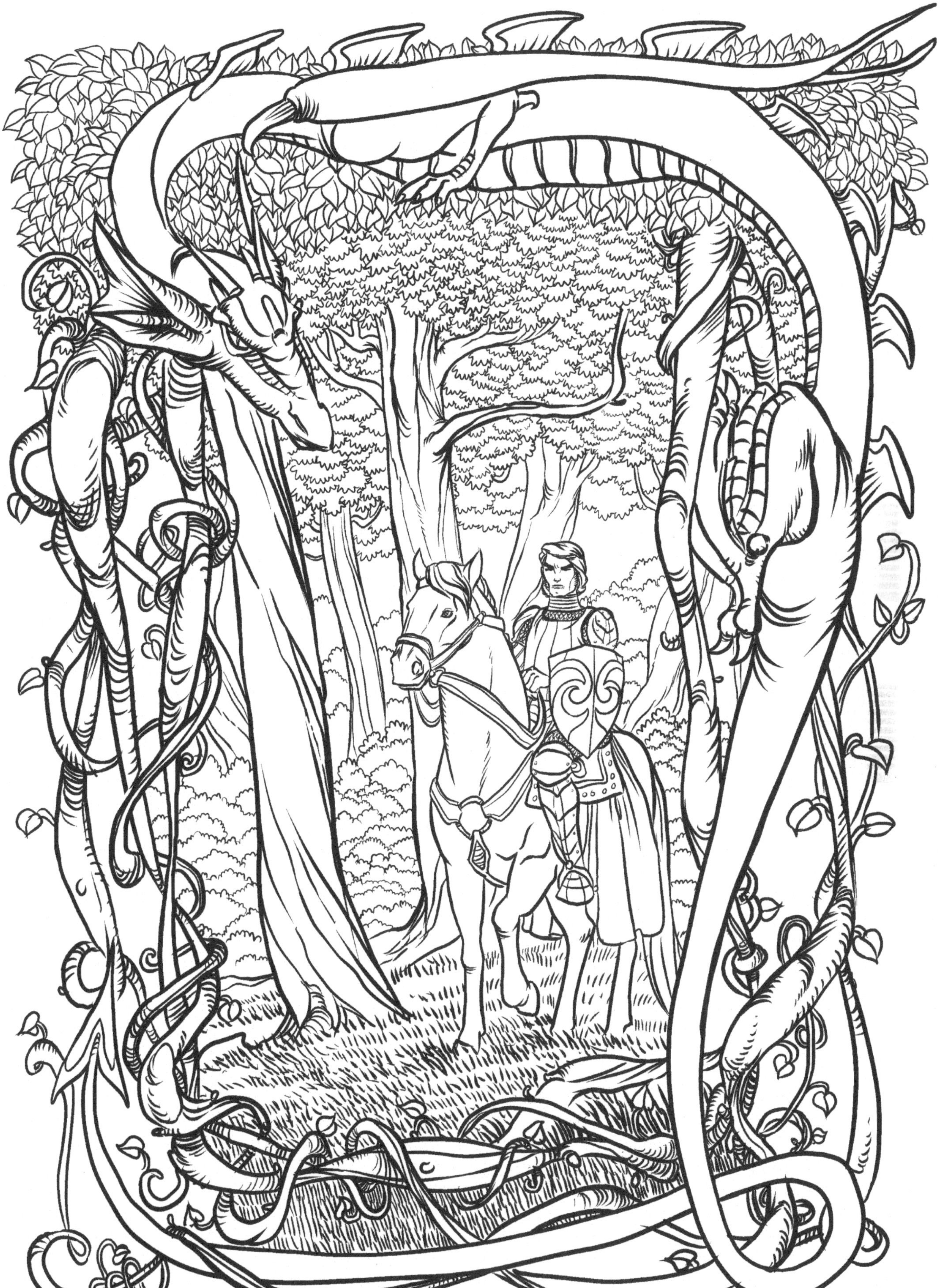

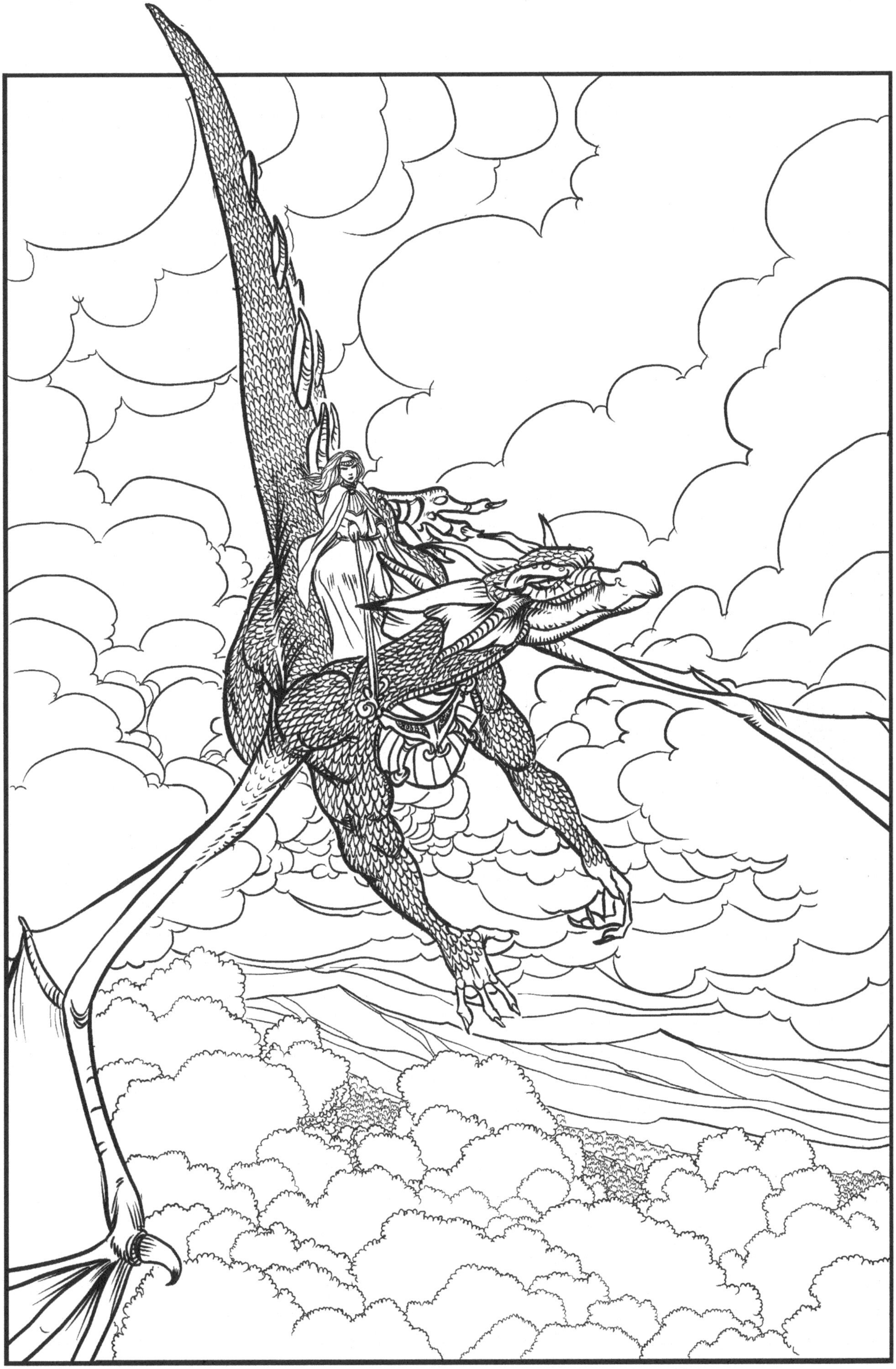

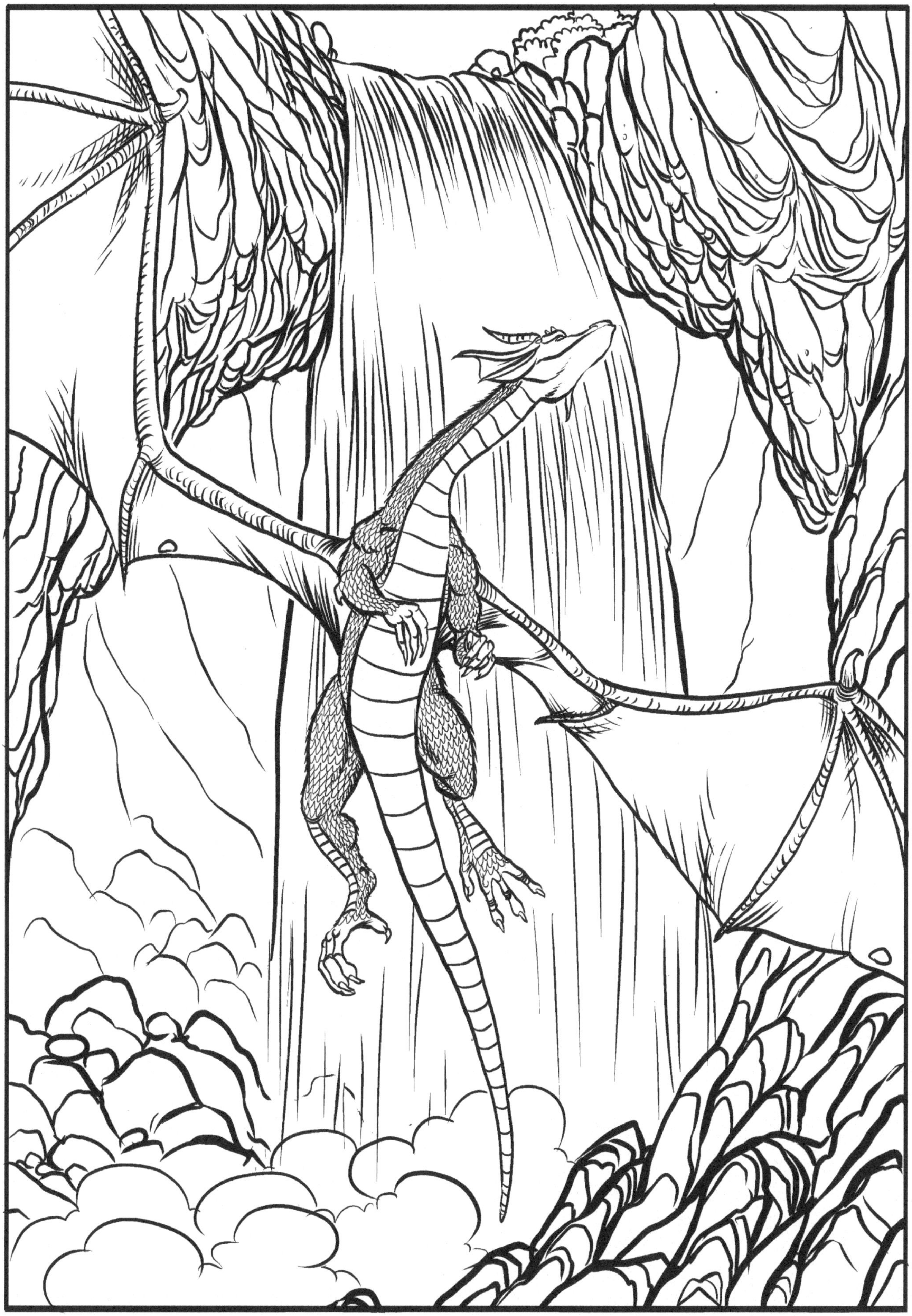

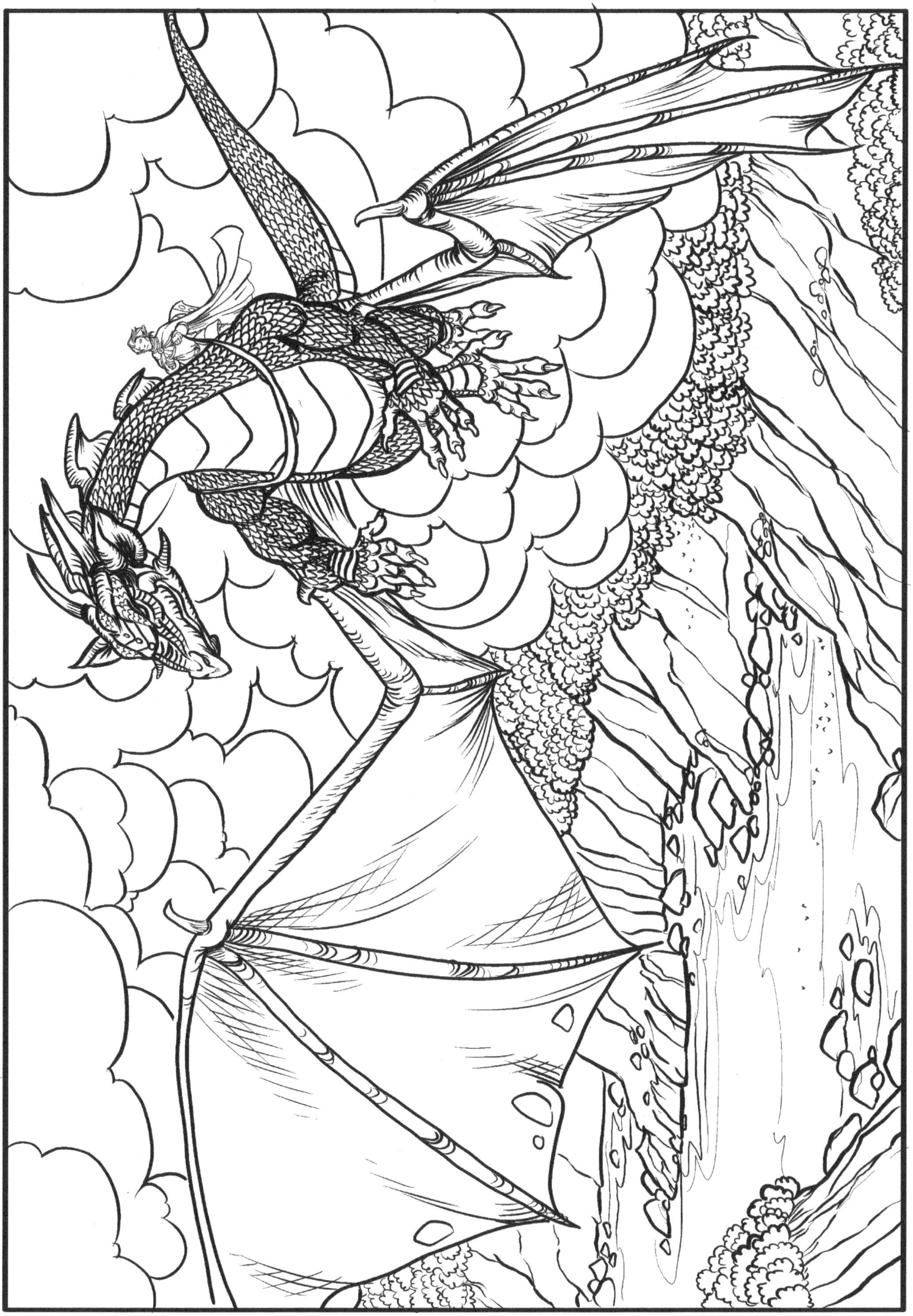

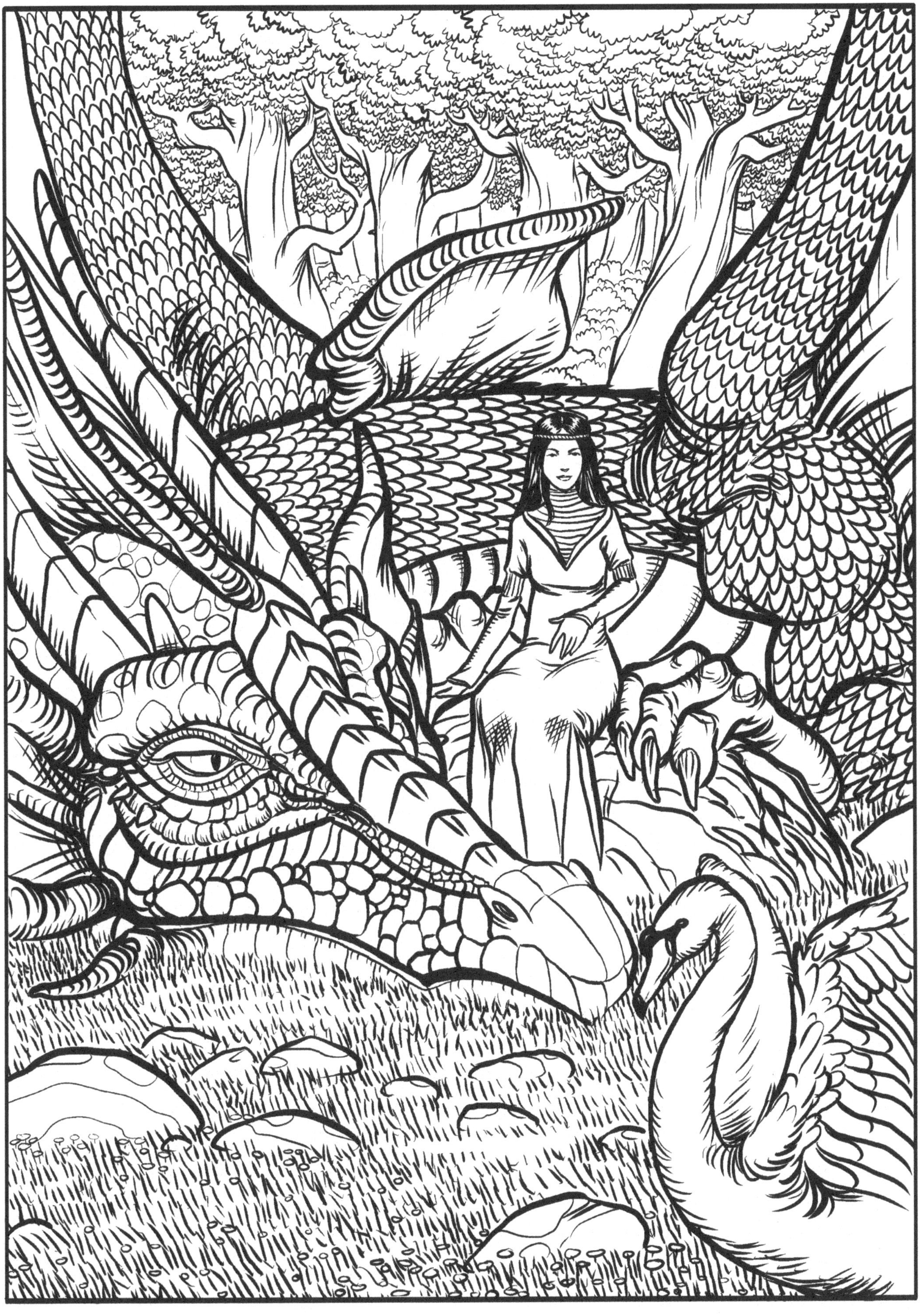

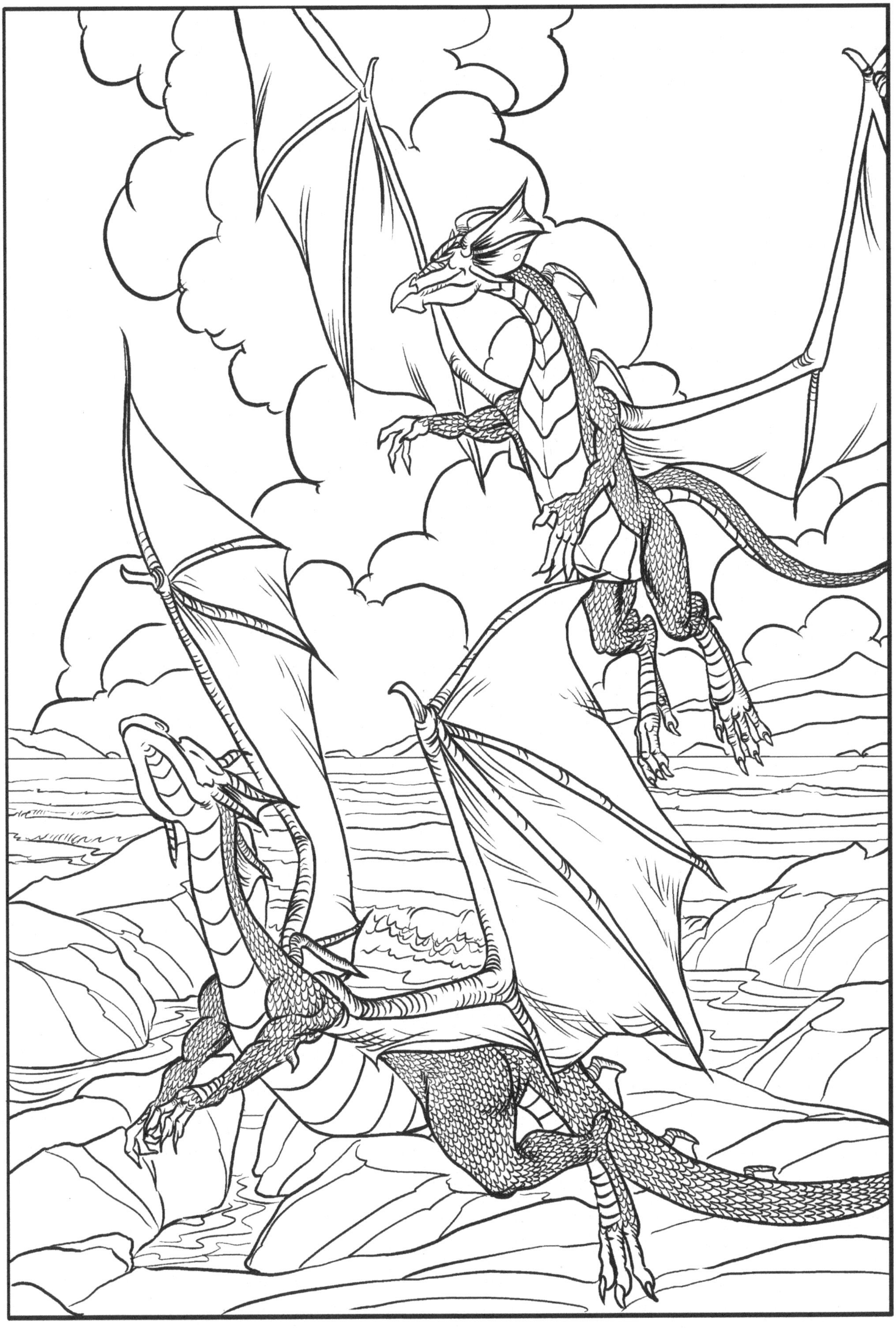

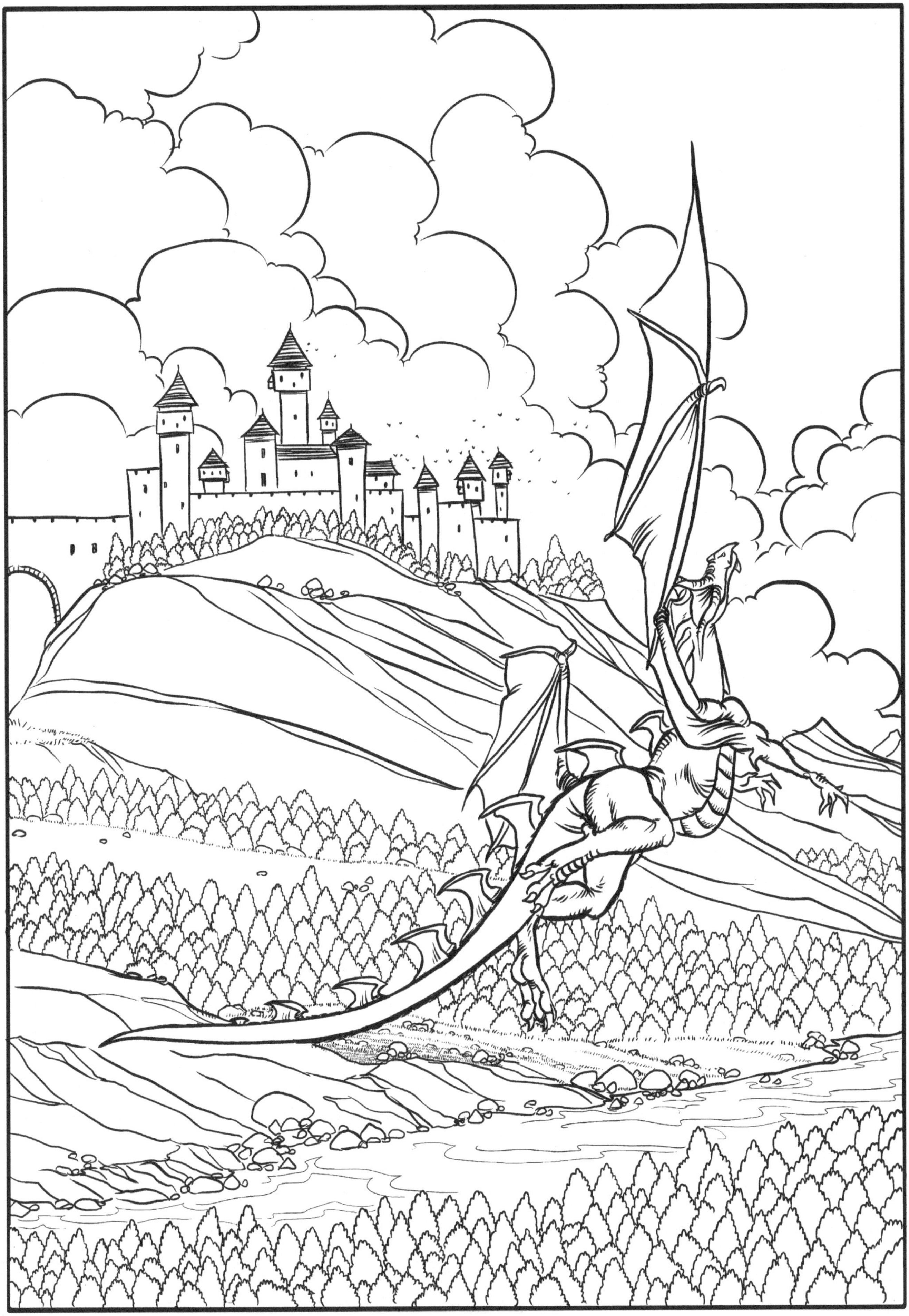

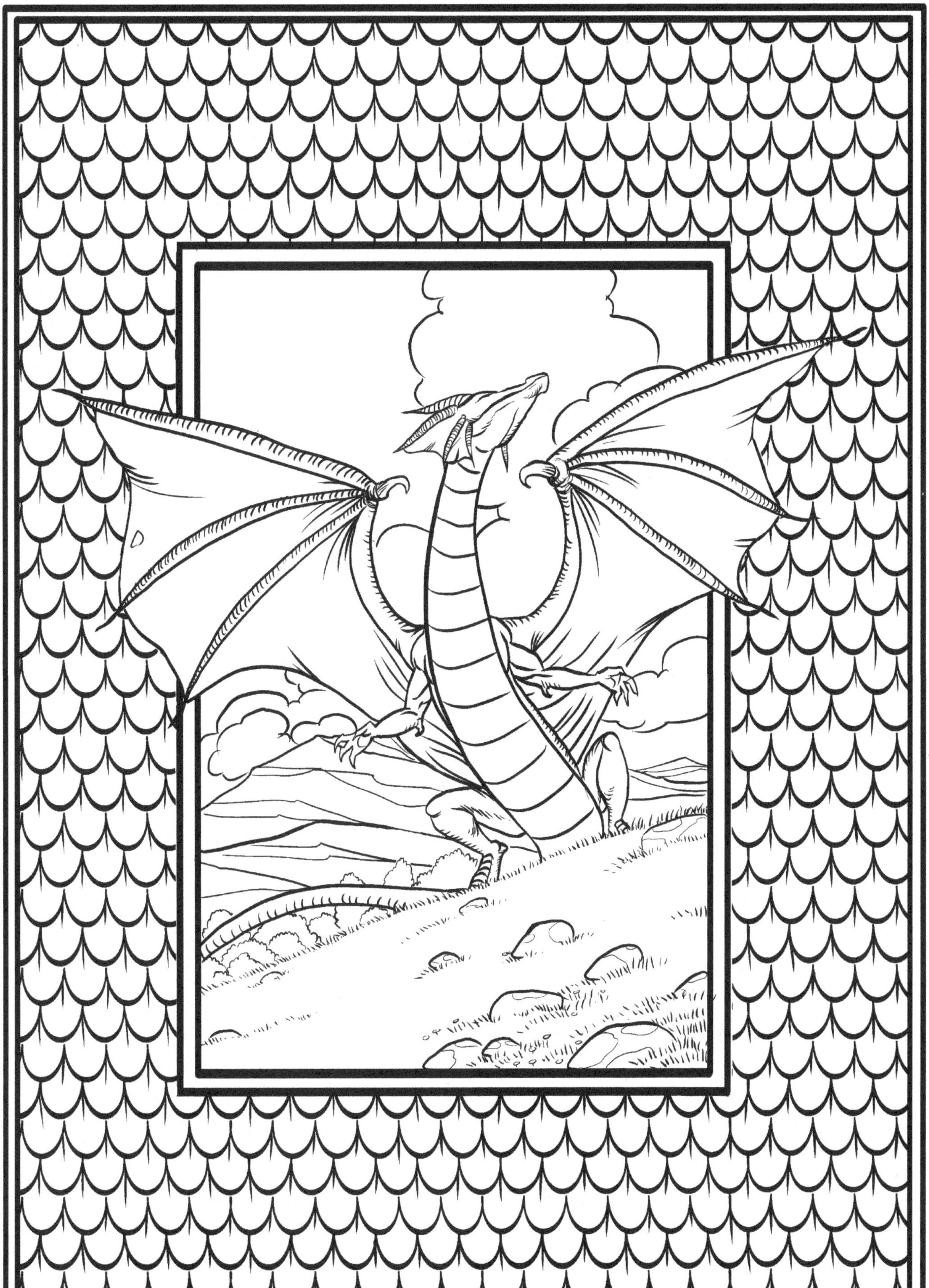

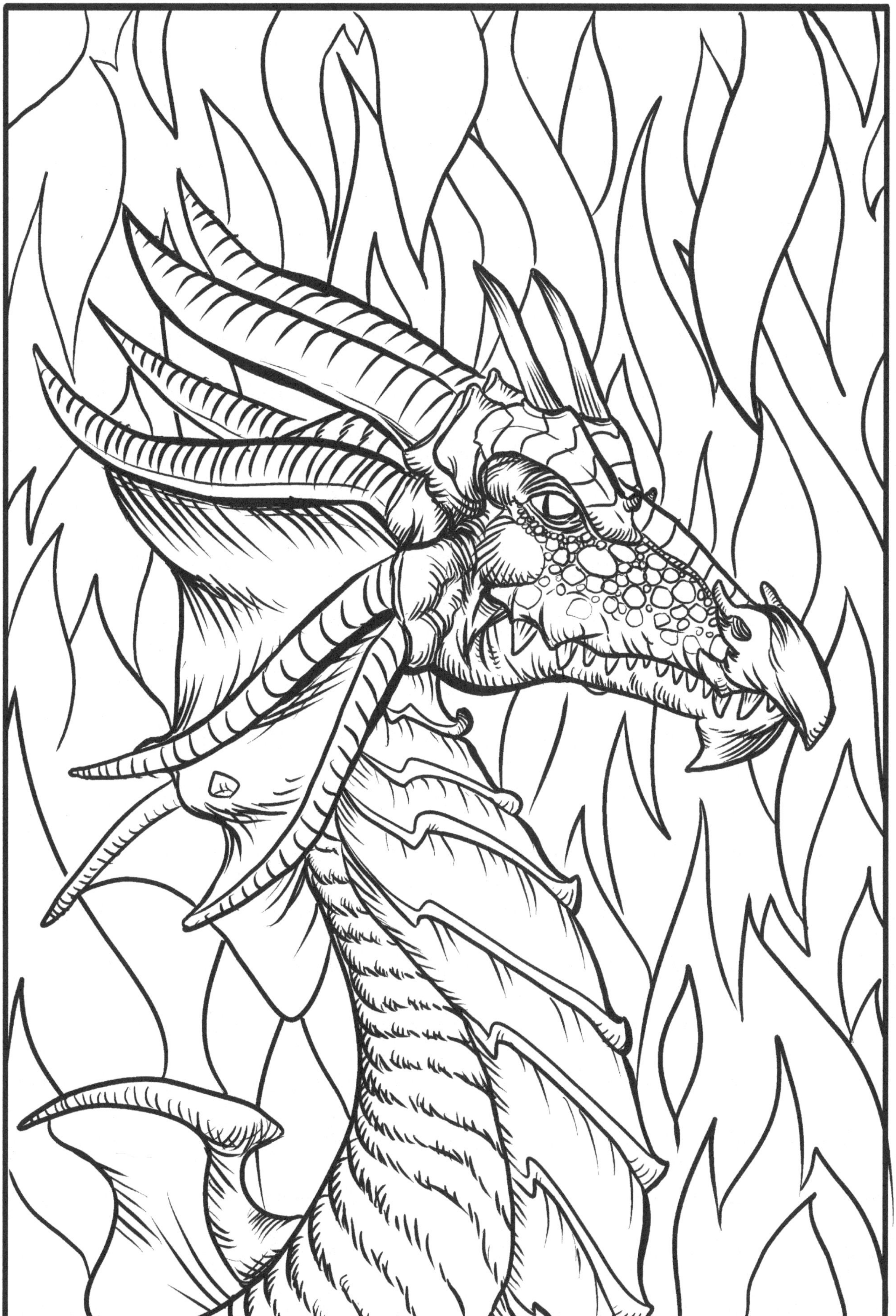

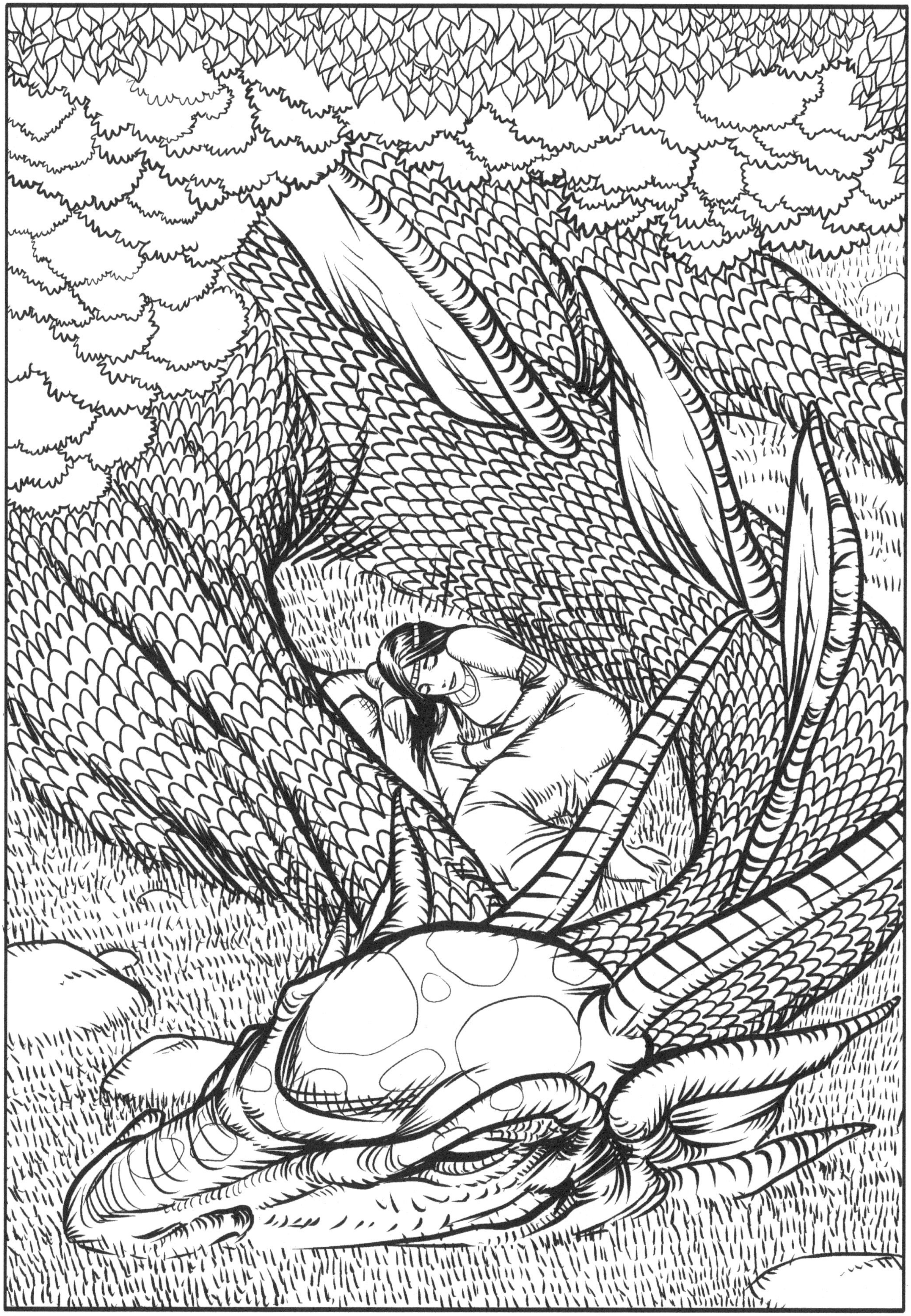

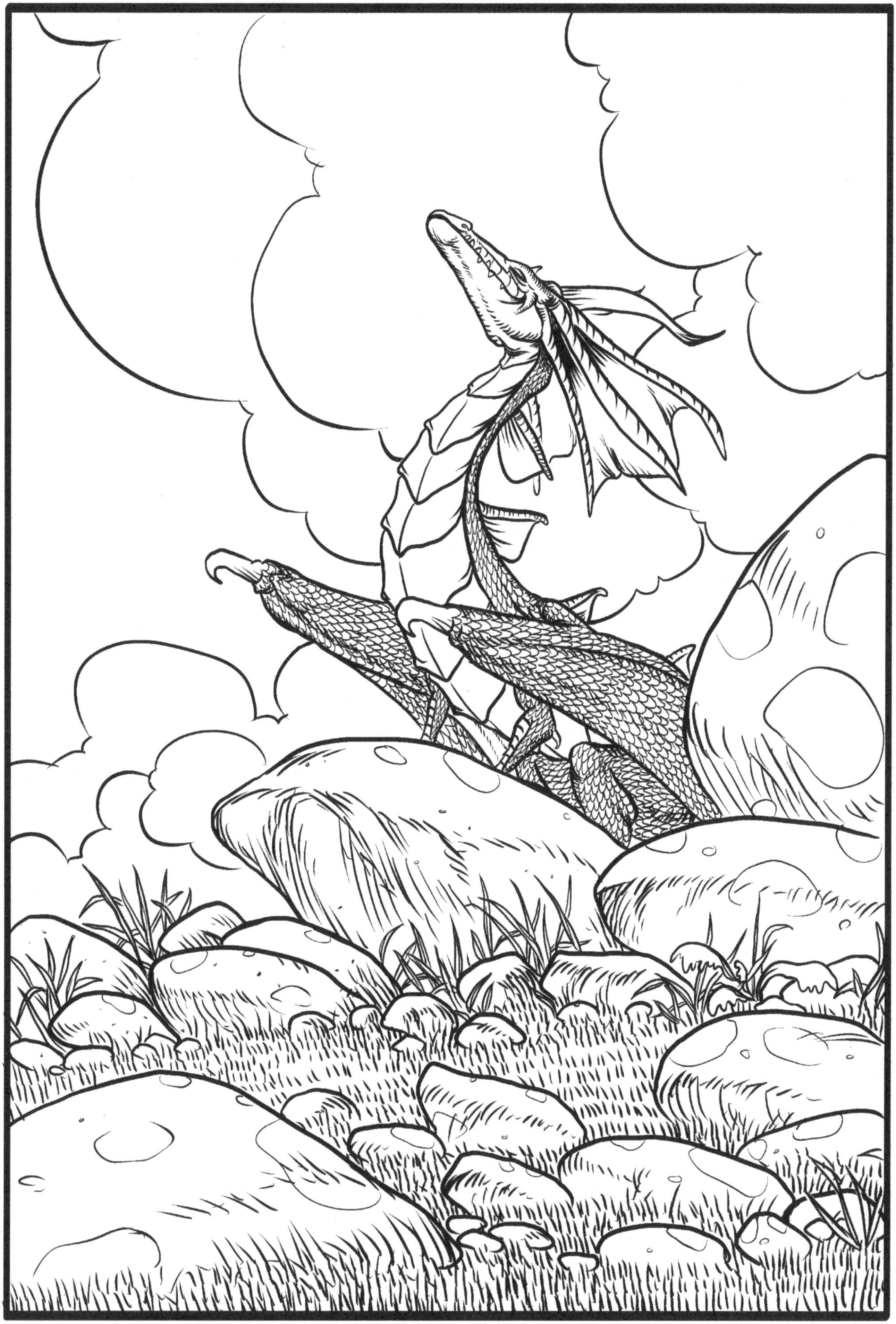

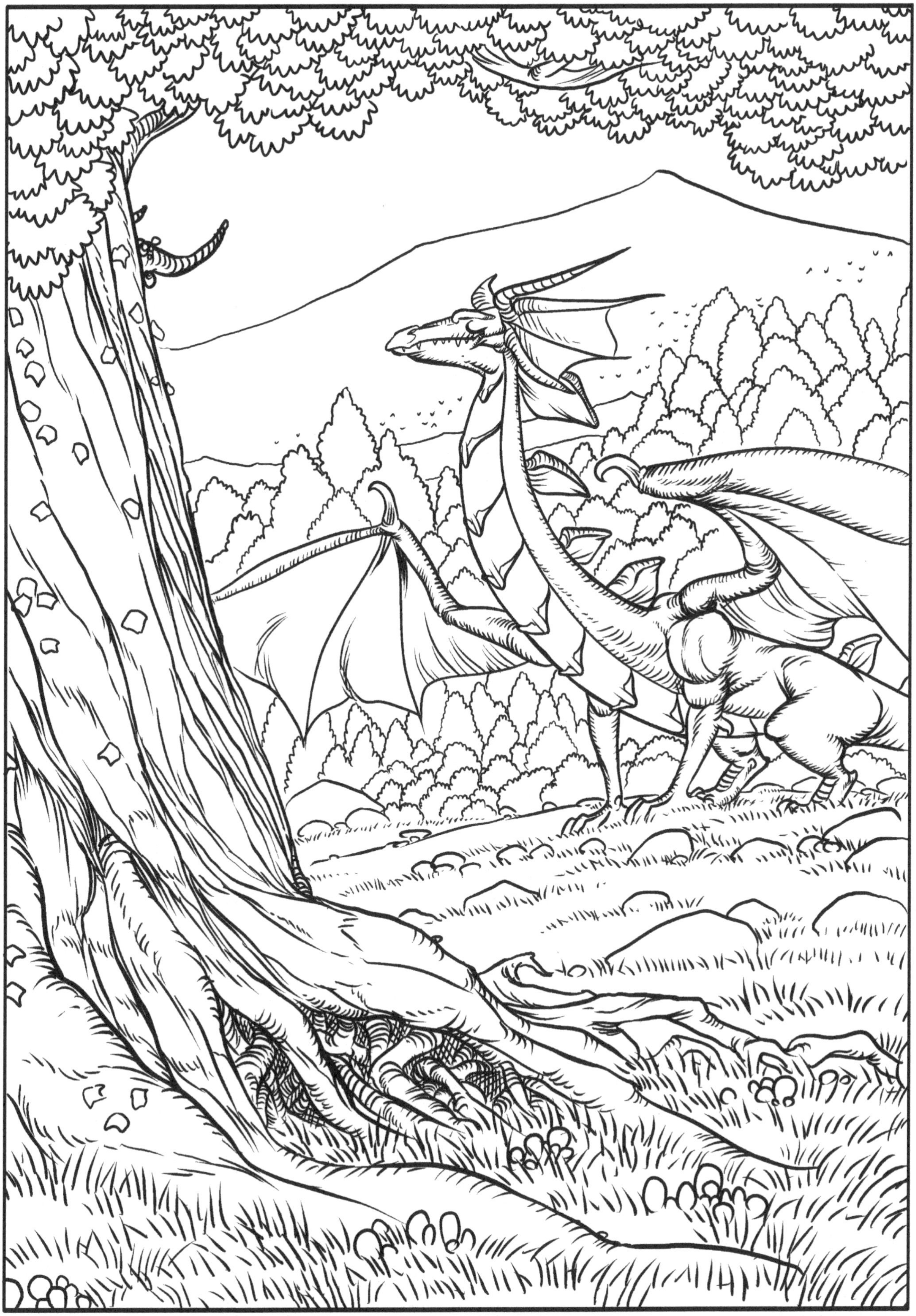

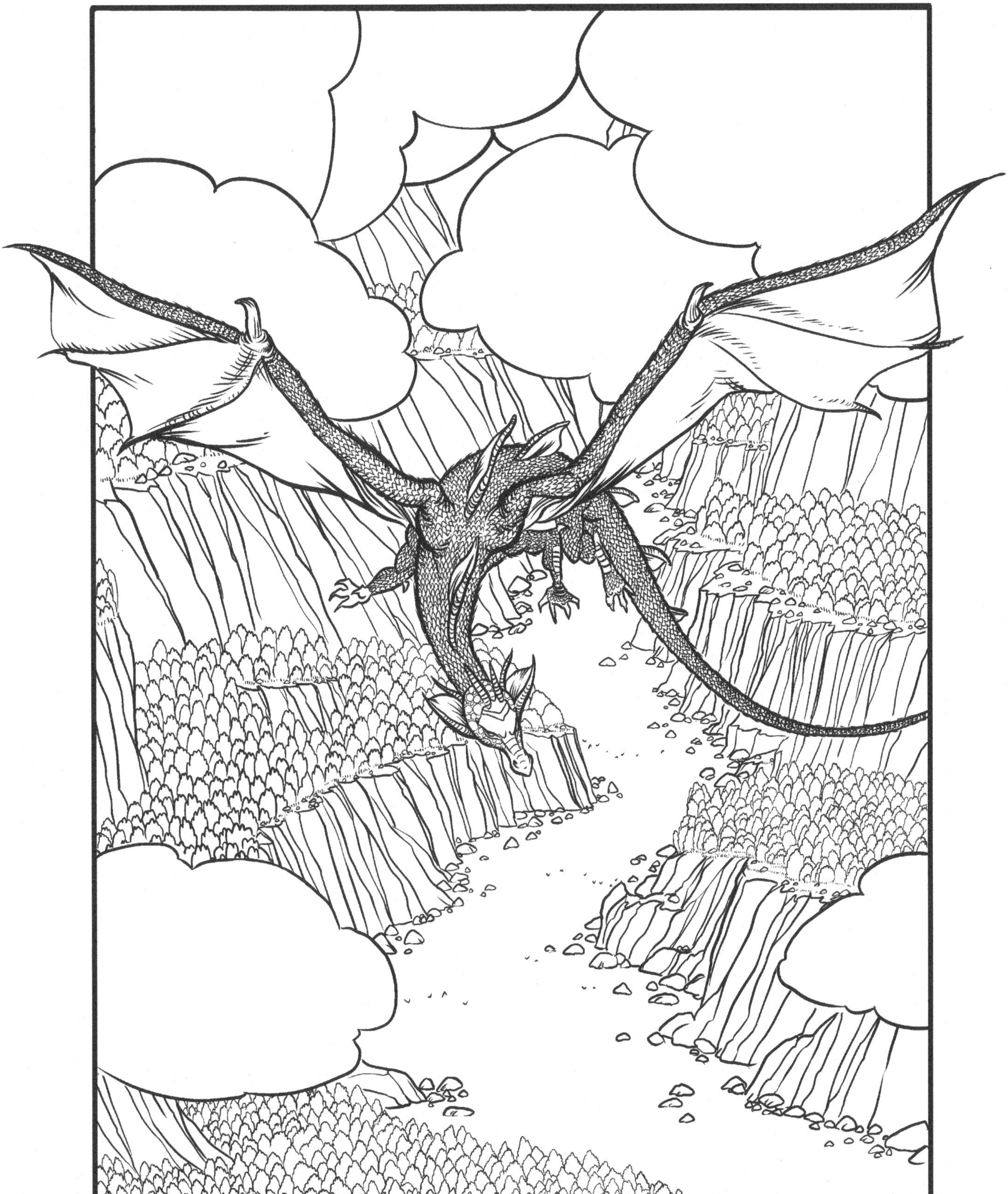

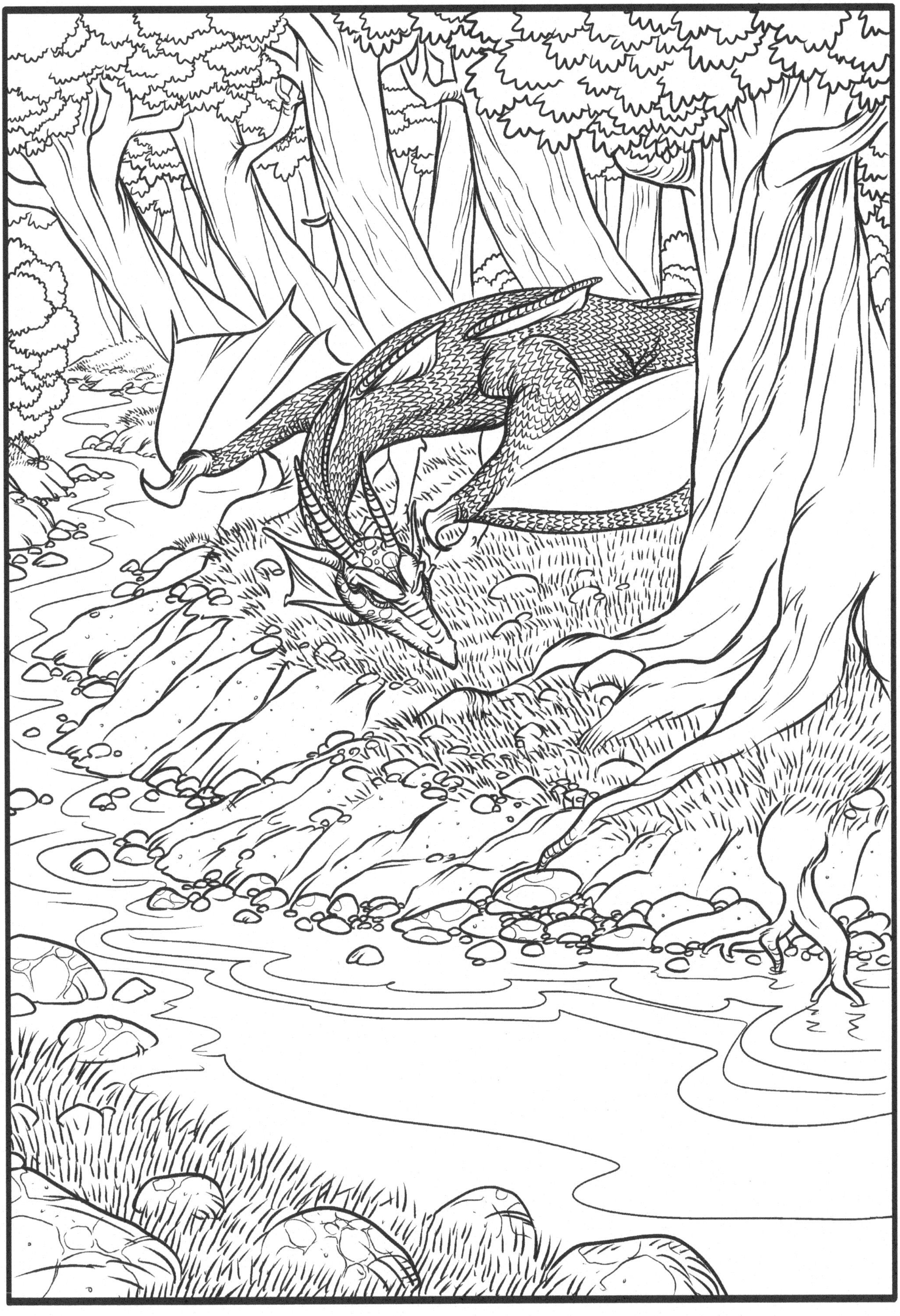

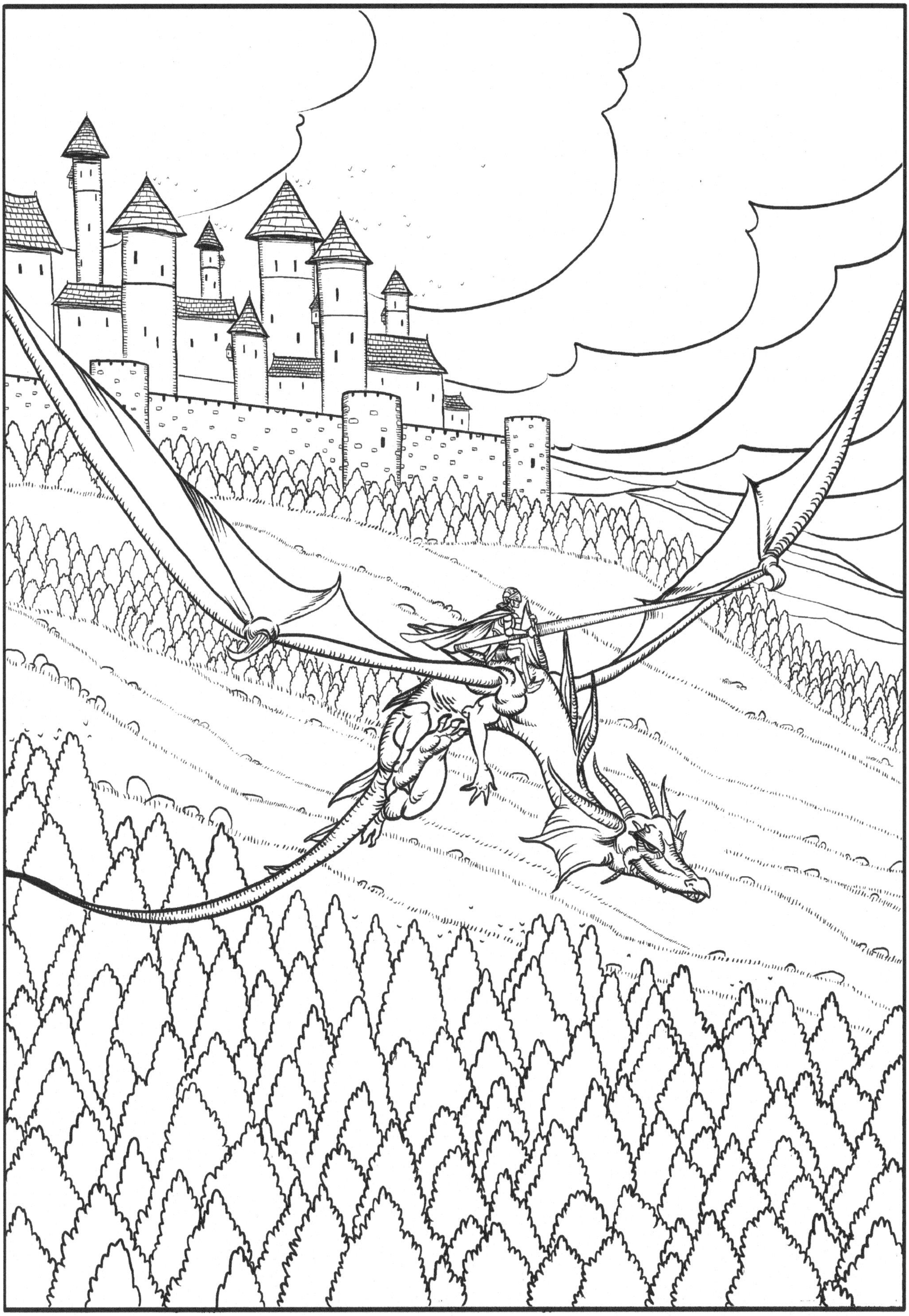

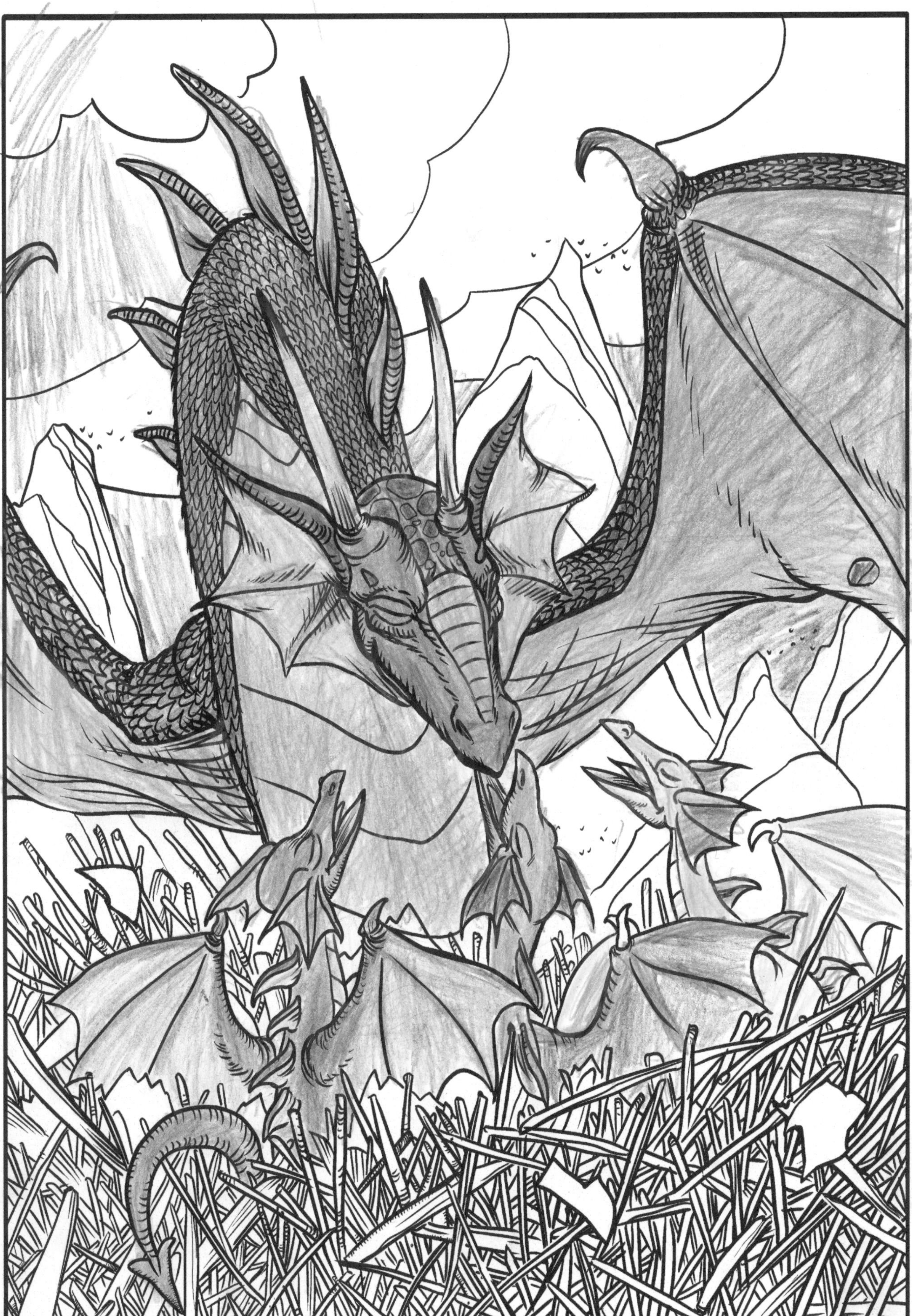

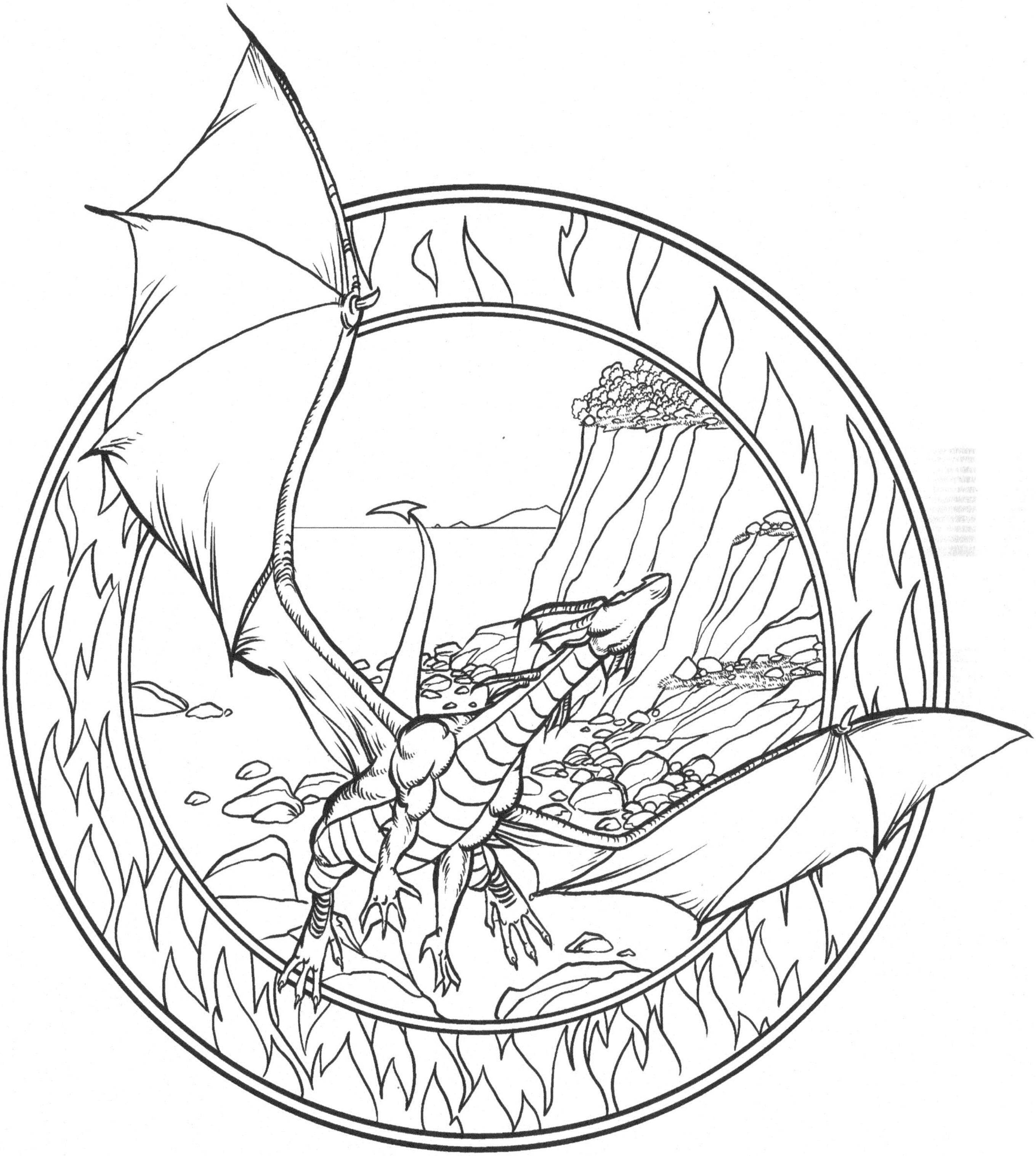

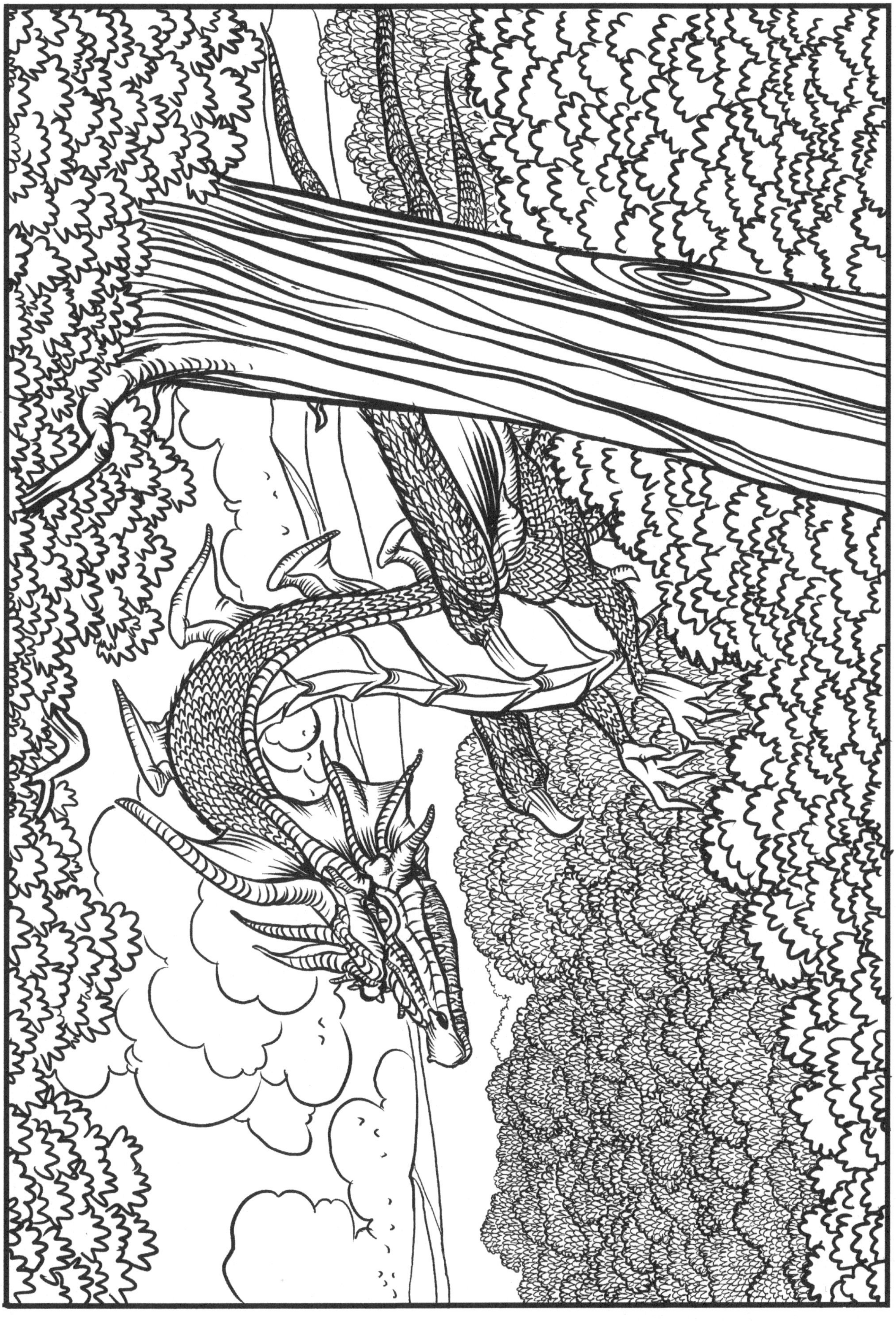